IN BLOOM

Francis Wootton's first memory is of Kurt Cobain's death. Since then, this would-be poet and possible intellectual (who is definitely wasted on Tyne and Wear) has grown used to figuring out life on his own. When he is diagnosed with leukaemia at fifteen, a whole new world of worry opens up. There's the horror of being held back a year at school; the threat of imminent baldness; having to locate his best shirt in case a visiting princess or pop star fancies a photo-op. But he hadn't reckoned on meeting fierce, tough, one-of-a-kind Amber — and finding a reason to tackle it all head-on . . .

Books by Matthew Crow
Published by Ulverscroft:

MY DEAREST JONAH

MATTHEW CROW

◆

IN BLOOM

Complete and Unabridged

ULVERSCROFT
Leicester

First published in Great Britain in 2013 by
Much-in-Little
an imprint of
Constable & Robinson Ltd
London

First Large Print Edition
published 2016
by arrangement with
Constable & Robinson Ltd
London

A catalogue record for this book is available from the British Library.

ISBN 978–1–4448–2721–7

Published by
F. A. Thorpe (Publishing)
Anstey, Leicestershire

Set by Words & Graphics Ltd.
Anstey, Leicestershire
Printed and bound in Great Britain by
T. J. International Ltd., Padstow, Cornwall

This book is printed on acid-free paper

Here's a test:

Leukaemia

Look at the word quickly then look away. Now, close your eyes and try to spell it. Bet you couldn't?

Neither could I.

Before

My first memory was of Kurt Cobain's death. I was four. Chris was thirteen. For three days all you could hear in our house was 'Smells Like Teen Spirit' and the sound of my brother howling in his bedroom.

'Sweetheart, I know it's difficult but life goes on,' Mum said.

'Not if you're dead.'

'For God's sake, Christopher, just get up.'

'No.'

'I'll pay you.'

'CAPITALIST!'

Mum was trying her hardest, but after he'd missed a whole week of school she just gave up. Within a year Chris had grown his hair long and announced to anyone who would listen that he was gay. This was Tyne and Wear. In 1994. People listened.

Like I said, that was my first memory. By the time I was fifteen, Chris was twenty-four. He lived not far from us, and came round at least twice a week with a new mix CD for me and an empty carrier bag, which he stuffed full of the contents of our fridge. Mum kicked off every time he did it, but I knew that whenever she was in Marks she bought double so that he wouldn't go hungry. She was nice like that, though Chris wouldn't admit it.

Also Dad didn't live with us any more. He didn't *not* live there — he just went away and didn't come back for really long stretches. The longest was the time he managed to miss both Chris's eighteenth *and* twenty-first birthdays. That was a low even by his standards.

Mum loved us in her own way. She loved Emma, my twin sister, too. People used to say just how like Mum Em looked. This was a compliment. Mum was beautiful. She was a model in London when she was my age. Apparently a journalist said that she had the next 'look'. Chris pretended it was embarrassing but I knew he showed old photos of her to his friends when he was drunk. He also told them how she could have been really famous, and how we could have grown up in London and been Bohemians, only one photographer asked her to go topless and when Grandma found out she got the first train to London and dragged Mum back, kicking and screaming. Mum didn't really talk about it any more. Grandma did. Every time she heard the *EastEnders* theme tune she reminded us of how a cockney tried to destroy her family's honour, and how over her dead body would he have got away with it, and how she was charged over a pound for a cup of tea at King's Cross . . .

Either way, Mum was beautiful and so was Emma. All children are supposed to be beautiful; they're not, though. Emma was beautiful, that was just the way it went. It was her thing.

One afternoon not long after she died, I remember sitting downstairs with Chris. Mum had been in bed for two days and we'd only had toast for tea and I asked him whether we were going to be taken into care.

'Mum still loves you. Just . . . from a distance.' Chris clocked my gormless expression and went on, 'When something bad happens you have to make sure you're more careful. She just needs to be a bit tougher now so nothing can hurt her the same way again. Once bitten and all that.'

This made more sense to me. I used to love dogs until Rebecca Speckman's Alsatian chased me through the back cut and sank its teeth into my left leg; ever since then just passing a dog on the street was enough to provoke a minor breakdown in me.

I put this to Chris and he nodded slowly, trying not to laugh.

'I suppose you're right, kidder,' he said,

and carried on smoking out of the window.

Mum always used to make a point of telling Emma and me what a lovely surprise we were. Chris (who at the time was going through a phase of listening to loud music and being a total shit) translated this for me.

'It means you were accidents,' he said, tugging on the sleeves of his Marilyn Manson hoodie and scanning me for a reaction.

He must have felt bad about it, though, because once he'd cheered up and gone back to listening to happy music by skinny boys with model girlfriends he made sure he corrected himself.

'Look, I didn't mean it,' he said. 'You weren't planned, is all. But it worked out OK . . . you were sort of like the fiver you find in your jeans after they've been through the wash.'

At this stage I was still on fifty pence a week pocket money. By the end of the year inflation would push me way over the pound mark. Regardless, the thought of being the equivalent of a whole fiver made me feel like the most special boy in the whole world.

Chris was tougher than me and had more of an accent. This was because when he was born Dad had just started working and Mum was still running her business from the back bedroom. They were pretty young, I suppose, by the standards of most parents. They lived on a street where they seemed to film quite a lot of *Crimestoppers*, two bus stops away from the house we later moved to. Chris went to the local comp. By the time I came along they had moved. Dad had his job and Mum had a proper office. They didn't send me to the comp, they sent me to a school where no one really had an accent. Chris moved schools too, for a little while, but for some reason he told his friends that he was at his old school all the way through.

Chris worked as a graphic designer. He stayed late at his office to make a magazine that nobody read, about bands that nobody listened to. I could say that and know I was not being cruel. Firstly because it was true, secondly because Chris said it first — I was simply repeating it.

★   ★   ★

After summer — when we returned to school for our final year — everything seemed different. Everybody was less certain. Every conversation involved change. Involved whatever would come next. Out of nowhere we had choice — whether we wanted to stay; whether we wanted to go; which subjects suited our interests. School became an option, and an exciting one at that. For those of us who were staying, parts of the building that never had been before would become accessible; the classes would become smaller; attendance would be up to us. We would even get to choose what we wore.

Those leaving would no longer be shut up within those same four walls. They would have to make new friends, see new people every day, unlearn the old rules and get to grips with the new ones. Nobody knew exactly what they were doing next. But everyone knew that they would be doing *something*. And even if that something was to choose to do nothing then the choice would be theirs, where it never had been before. Something was ending. And something was beginning. Nobody quite knew what was coming, but we knew it would be huge. Nothing seemed certain any more, nothing seemed static or un-doable; it felt like a reward, like after fifteen years life was finally opening up for us.

1

When my headaches started Mum took me to the optician's.

'It'll be your eyes. It's always the eyes. They always think it's not, but it is,' she said as she pulled me along the street, dodging the people handing out flyers for free makeovers, and the others asking for two minutes of her time to save the tigers and stop the war with a small monthly direct debit.

The optician lowered the giant binoculars to my face and turned the lights down low. He put different lenses into the goggles and kept asking about the fuzzy alphabet on the wall in front of me.

'Better or worse?' he said as he checked his digital watch in the dark.

'Can I ask a question?' I said.

'Can you just read the letters first?'

'Yes. A, B, P, H, Q, V, S, T, M, O, then maybe an X, but I'm not quite sure.'

He made a note.

'Are we comparing to the last time or the first time?' I said.

'What?'

'Am I saying it's better or worse than the

very first time with no glass in at all, or better or worse than the one that just went before? Only I'm not quite sure which you mean.'

'The one before.'

'Oh. I can't remember. Can I try again?'

He puffed out his breath and changed the lens.

'Better,' I said eventually. 'I remember now. Definitely better.'

'Very good,' he said, and fiddled with the knobs either side of the binoculars. 'Now once more . . . read as far as you can go and let me know if it's better or worse.'

'I have one more question,' I said eventually. Your eyes are vital; I needed to get this right.

The optician sighed loudly.

'Than the last time, Francis,' he snapped, with a little more emotion than I felt appropriate for a health practitioner.

'Just checking.'

★   ★   ★

It wasn't my eyes, it turned out.

'God knows what it is,' Mum said as we made our way to Marks for coffee and a scone. 'You haven't been smoking, have you? Oh, God, it's not drugs, is it? Francis, you can talk to me, you know? Francis . . . I will find out.'

Obviously she wouldn't. I could be quite

deceitful when the mood took me. I once had two off a joint at a party of Chris's and she was none the wiser.

'No, it's not drugs. I hardly even drink.'

'*Hardly?*'

'Only when you let me.'

'Hmmmm. Well, just let me know it if gets any worse,' she said, draining her cappuccino.

★   ★   ★

When we got to Grandma's house I presented her with a handful of sugar sachets that I'd swiped from the café.

'Cheers, flower,' she said, lunging towards me, kissing my cheek and grabbing the slack handful, which she deposited into the front pocket of her apron.

'I really don't appreciate you getting him to steal for you. He's enough on with his GCSEs as it is without petty theft complicating things,' said Mum. 'If you want sugar, I'll bloody well buy you it,' she added, dropping Grandma's carriers in the hall and making her way to the kitchen.

'*Julie,*' Grandma said, '*the language.*'

Grandma's house had the atmosphere of a Tupperware box left out in the sun. Like a tropical flower, she had to be kept warm and moist at all times, or she would wilt and die.

'Besides, I like the sachets. Saves you having to wash a tea-spoon. I just pour it in and I'm away.'

'*Oh?*' Mum said. 'Away where, exactly? The bowls club for an orange squash? Or the pharmacist for that repeat prescription? Or just up the top to catch the post? Those saved minutes must be a real godsend.'

'My little ray of sunshine, eh?' Grandma said, cupping my cheek in her hand. After they'd unpacked the shopping we sat down for a bit. Grandma turned the TV to its lowest setting as Mum filled her in on my ailments. I sat quietly, concentrating hard on not throwing up by lip-reading the commentary on the horse racing.

'Anaemia,' Grandma concluded. 'You can see it in his face. Dark circles. He's losing weight too. Though it doesn't surprise me . . . '

'Don't!' Mum said.

She and Grandma never quite saw eye to eye on anything. Take food, for instance. Grandma liked things to be brown and steaming and caked in pastry. Mum bought recipe magazines which Grandma said cost more than a week's shop should in the first place. Once, when Mum treated us to a meal for Chris's birthday, Grandma shrieked at the top of her voice when the waiter explained

12

what sushi was. Then Mum shrieked when Grandma sent it back and asked them to fry it. Even Chris looked embarrassed when she asked the waiter for some salt and vinegar. I can see both sides of the coin and play it to my advantage. With Mum I got essential vitamins and minerals, which were good for my skin and stimulated growth (being three inches below average height was no joke). Then at Grandma's I got the sort of food that always made it feel like a Sunday. She was never too busy to steam a pudding.

'Well, a lad can't grow big and strong off salad and fish.'

'We eat perfectly healthily.'

'He needs a plate mince pie, some Cadbury's Smash, and half a tin of peas. That'll sort him out,' Grandma said, and nodded once.

That was the last that was said on the subject.

★　★　★

At the door we kissed her goodbye.

'WAIT!' she yelled, running back inside.

'Now what?' Mum said, clicking the car open with the remote key. 'Oh, come on, let's just go before she gets back.'

'One minute,' Grandma hollered from the back kitchen.

When she came back she was all out of breath and carrying something in her hand.

'Here.'

She slapped a wet package into Mum's hands. It looked like brains in a pick-and-mix bag.

'Jesus Christ!' said Mum as mince juice began leaking between her fingers and on to the cuff of her jacket.

'Promise me you'll feed him up. Get his strength back,' Grandma said as we walked towards the car.

She stood in the doorway waving as we pulled away.

'*Remember!*' Grandma yelled down the street. '*Half fat to flour!*'

Mum tooted once and stuck her hand out of the window as we turned the corner.

'Here,' she said, tossing the packet of mince towards me. As it flopped into my lap a bloody smear appeared across the front of my T-shirt. I looked like Jackie cradling JFK's brains.

'I swear to God,' said Mum, 'the sooner we convince them she has Alzheimer's, the better.'

★ ★ ★

Outside Chris's flat Mum lugged the Henry Hoover from the boot.

'How you feeling?' she asked me, puffing and red-faced as the cord got caught in the boot and she yanked it free.

'Fine. Just a bit sick.'

'Hmm.'

She held my face up to the light and I had to squint.

'Your glands aren't swollen. Let me know if it gets any worse. When did you last have some painkillers?'

'I think it was two hours ago, but it was on an empty stomach so I'd better leave it for now. The stated dose is two every three hours.'

'Well then, help me with this,' she said, handing me the vacuum.

We lugged it up Chris's path and Mum had to knock three times before anyone responded. I heard Fiona yelling from the flat followed by what sounded like a boulder rolling down the stairs. Eventually the door opened and she stood there in her underwear and one of Chris's shirts.

'Morning.'

'It's quarter to three,' Mum said.

Fiona's hair hadn't been washed or brushed and she had bruises on her knees. I should at this stage point out that I loved Fiona with all of my heart and had a sneaking suspicion she felt the same way, only was too frightened to do anything about it. I wasn't being deluded, either. I had three pieces of concrete evidence to suggest as much.

One: of all Chris's flatmates who I knew liked me (Fiona, Callum and Dan) and the one I wasn't so sure about (Beth), Fiona was the only one who bought me a Christmas present. One year it was a battered old Beatles LP, and the year before that a stack of eighties porn magazines she'd found at a flea market. Grandma took a funny turn on Boxing Day when she asked to have a look at my *Beano* annual.

Two: although I think she probably fancied Chris first, he was gay so she had little to no chance of ever begetting children with him. Genetically speaking I was next best thing, only with the advantage of a slightly increased life expectancy due to my tender years.

Three: once, at a New Year's Eve party, I had gone to bed to read after we'd all said Happy New Year, and Fiona came into the bedroom about half an hour later and passed out next to me, using a guest's coat for a blanket. When she told me she felt sick I went to get a bucket to put next to the bed, and before she nodded back off she said she loved me. I knew she was drunk, but I believed that in this instance alcohol had allowed her to shed her inhibitions and speak from the heart.

16

We were obviously destined to be together.

'Julie, always a pleasure,' she said, standing aside in the doorway to let us in.

'You look like you've been exhumed,' Mum told her.

'That crease in your trousers is particularly succinct today.'

'Do you want the Hoover or not?'

'Not particularly but needs must.'

Mum and Fiona always had little jokes like this.

'Hi, hot stuff,' Fiona said, and grabbed me in a tight hug as I walked inside. She smelled of perfume and whisky. 'I'm hanging like you wouldn't believe here, can you help?'

I hugged her back and dug out some chewing gum from my pocket.

'It'll stimulate saliva which might help dehydration. And sugar's supposed to be good for a hangover,' I said. She took the chewing gum and put a piece in her shirt pocket.

'You are a curious one, Francis, a real find.'

Fiona made jokes like this with me all the time too. I didn't entirely understand them, but was happy to play along regardless.

Mum made her way up the stairs with the Hoover and before we reached the landing we heard her yelling.

'Bloody hell, Christopher, it looks like Basra in here!'

The rest of the household groaned.

'*Volume!*' Chris said.

'No sympathy.' Mum began rolling the Hoover to the farthest corner of the room. Fiona came in carrying a whole bar of Dairy Milk and a blanket. She kicked Callum's legs off the couch and sat down beside him, making a show of squishing herself deeper and deeper into the recesses of the couch.

'Do you want some chocolate, Francis?' she asked, brandishing the bar at me from her nest.

'No, thanks, we had lunch in town.'

'I remember a time when I used to have lunch,' she said, pretending to be sad, and started munching her way through the chocolate. 'Now it's all Red Cross parcels and harvest festival donations.'

'Speaking of which . . . here!' Mum threw the plastic bag of mince towards Chris. 'Courtesy of Grandma.'

'Thanks. I suppose,' he said, examining the entrails.

Callum's eyes widened. He shifted on the sofa, pressing himself backwards like a shocked kitten, and for the first time since we'd arrived sat bolt upright. Then he lurched towards the door.

'Going to throw up!' he said, only just making it to the bathroom before the sound

18

of damp retching started to echo off the porcelain bowl.

'Charming. Look, we're not stopping because we've got things to do,' said Mum, widening her eyes at me, which meant it was time to go.

'How you feeling now?' Chris asked me.

'Fine, I suppose. The optician said I had twenty-twenty vision, which means I could become a pilot or join the army, if the mood ever takes me.'

'Worth the trip then,' he said.

'I love a man in uniform,' said Fiona, sprawling over Callum's place on the sofa and resting her head gently in Beth's lap.

On the mantelpiece, between the full ashtrays and the well-thumbed stacks of takeaway leaflets, sat a pile of letters. They had been there, unopened, for as long as I could remember, but for some reason they seemed to pique Mum's interest.

'What are these?' she asked, going over and picking one of them up.

'Private correspondence,' said Chris, taking the letter off her.

'Counc-LOL-tax,' said Fiona, retreating ever further into the sofa.

'They'll take you to court, you know. You'll get a record.'

'*We shall overcome!*' said Chris sarcastically.

'Well, don't think I'll be posting bail when they lock you up. Honestly, the money I spent on your education, and even life's most basic skills are beyond you. And the state of this place . . . '

'Enter Henry Hoover.'

'Well, you do have to plug him in and use him, you know,' Mum said. 'Just having him here won't make any difference.'

Chris grabbed a notepad and pen and pretended to scribble down her instructions.

'*Plug in . . . push . . .* think I've just about got the gist.'

'I don't know why I bother,' Mum said, kissing his forehead and slipping him £20 before we left.

Just as we were about to go Callum came out of the toilet, looking hunched and sad, like he was too delicate to handle anything bad life might throw at him. He squinted up at us and his whole body spasmed once more as he noticed something on my face.

'Oh, God!' he said, with his fingers pressed to his mouth, and ran back towards the toilet.

'Are you all right?' Chris asked me, standing up from his place on the floor. He took me by the arm and sat me down as Mum rummaged through her bag for something. She came at me with a packet of Kleenex and a worryingly determined look in her eyes.

20

I still didn't entirely know what was going on until I felt something warm trace the length of my lip and spread down my chin, and then gulped down on a glob of metallic-tasting blood.

'AAAAAAAAAH!' I screamed from the couch.

'You have to apply pressure,' Mum said, with her iron fingers crushing the bridge of my nose like a torturer. 'Or it won't clot.'

'Just let it bleed!' I begged.

'Shut up, Francis, she knows what she's doing,' Chris told me.

'See?' Mum said, pressing harder on my nose.

'Oh, my God, it *hurts*!'

'Don't be so soft.'

'You're fracturing my skull!'

'Man up, Francis,' said Fiona from the couch.

I steeled myself and tried to be more macho about the ordeal. But Mum was tough. No matter how fancily she dressed, she couldn't hide her true nature. Everyone at school was scared of her. Especially the other mums. She once knocked out a man with a single punch when he barged her trolley in Sainsbury's. She also went round to Scott Earnshaw's house when Chris told her about his campaign of terror against me.

When Scott's mum tried to deny it was happening, Mum gave her a final warning. After Scott didn't heed her advice and locked me in the art cupboard one lunchtime, Mum went back to their house and lunged at Mrs Earnshaw. Chris and I watched from the car but they landed inside the vestibule and Mum kicked the door shut with her leg. When Chris asked her what the hell she was playing at, she just smiled and said, '*Reverting to type.*' Then we drove to McDonald's and had a drive-thru. I marked it in my diary at the time as 'The Best Day Ever'.

★　★　★

After five solid minutes of the sort of pain they make documentaries about Mum eased her grip a bit.

'There, I think that got it,' she said, standing up and observing her handiwork.

My nose felt like it was about to drop off. I was scared to touch it, and doubly scared to look in case of irreversible damage. I'd already had it broken once and feared the worst. My eyes were watering and I could feel myself weaken with the trauma of it all.

'Do you want a T-shirt to change into?' Chris said.

I nodded feebly and he told me to help myself. Only as I got up I saw him and Mum give each other a secret glance, which I knew meant they had been talking about me in private.

I took ages choosing a T-shirt that I wanted because Chris spent all his money shopping on eBay so borrowing clothes from him was much better than buying new ones from a shop. I saw two I liked. I put on the smallest underneath a Kiss T-shirt I'd had my eye on for some time, and dropped £2 into Chris's money jar, so it wasn't really stealing. While I was getting changed I could hear Mum and him talking about me in serious voices, only they stopped once I came out of his bedroom and Chris told me he would force-feed me the Kiss T-shirt if anything bad happened to it. I promised to take care of it. We left my T-shirt in his living room because Mum said it was ruined.

'Just cut off the bloody part and use it for dusting,' she told him when he protested.

He looked sick as anything but couldn't be bothered to argue.

★   ★   ★

'What were you and Chris talking about in the hallway?' I asked in the car on the way home.

'Just chatting,' said Mum, and pressed her foot to the floor.

'This is a thirty-miles-per-hour zone.'

'I can read, Francis.'

'In two years' time I'll be driving,' I said.

I had to keep doing this with Mum. She'd once promised me that for my seventeenth she would book me in on a booster block of driving lessons, so that fourteen days from my birthday I would be a qualified driver. It was up to me to maintain the momentum until she made good on her pledge. I imagined myself with Fiona in an open-topped sports car. The wind was blowing attractively through our hair as we cruised down country lanes, one of her hands resting casually on my leg. The only downsides were I'm not too great with directions, and the fact that there weren't many country lanes near ours. There was a patch of farmland and some hedges on the back road behind Asda, but it didn't look anything like my fantasy, more the sort of place that the *Evening Chronicle* describes as a 'Dogging Hotspot' (which I knew about because Mr and Mrs Tilsdale at number sixteen got done for it twice in one year). So that was my plan, and in preparation for it I had already bought a pair of mock-leather driving gloves and created the perfect mix tape for our sepia-toned journeys of love.

'We'll see,' Mum muttered to me.

'We will,' I said, putting one of Chris's mix CDs into the radio.

'Wahwahwah!' Mum said, rolling her eyes. 'Why do you always listen to this dirge?'

'It's cool.'

'It's depressing! In my day we only listened to music you could dance to. You're not going to bump and grind to some be-quiffed postgrad with a three-chord refrain and a broken heart,' she said, veering quickly sideways when she nearly missed the turnoff.

'You can shuffle to it, and sort of bounce your head while you're staring at the floor. Then you can pretend you're in a Cure video.'

'Even the Cure don't pretend they're in the Cure any more. Put on something more upbeat, Francis.'

'After this song. What were you talking about, with Chris? You didn't answer me before.'

'Oh . . . ' Mum said, driving faster and faster. 'Just making sure he was OK for money.'

'You said my name.'

She had, I'd been listening at the door.

'You may have cropped up in our conversation, yes, but only in passing. You're really not the most gripping of topics, love.'

As she spoke Mum poked her hand out of the car window and flipped her middle finger at a man in a Mondeo who had tooted at us twice. Then she went quiet and sighed.

'I do love you. You know that, Francis?'

'I know,' I said. 'I love you too.'

'Good,' she said, and nodded, speeding up even more as the traffic lights went from green to amber. 'Glad we got that sorted. Now change this song before it kills us both.'

2

It all came to a head on a Monday morning. The tests and the diagnosis and the strange, eerie dinners where there seemed to be a million things Mum and I wanted to say, but couldn't because we were pretending to listen to every single syllable the newsreader was uttering.

When I started feeling unwell she had tried to diagnose me herself. I knew she was doing it because she'd close the laptop every time I went into the front room then keep behaving strangely the next day. At first she thought I might have gastric flu because of the amount of time I spent in the bathroom. I played along for a while, but in truth I was in there for personal reasons. Mum was not one of life's 'knockers', and consequently all self-exploration had to be done behind the bathroom's bolted door.

Then she figured it might be an allergy of some sort, so she threw out all the toiletries and replaced them with white bars of soap that said soap-free on the packet (!?).

We were on nothing but meat and vegetables for a fortnight until she got sick of it and bought two loaves of sliced white and a frozen lasagne from the corner shop.

Then she thought it was depression so she took the lock off the bathroom door and left a leaflet about 'talking therapy' on my pillow one night while I was asleep. Eventually she took Grandma's advice and started doling out iron supplements before school every morning, which had a negative effect on my stomach and caused an almost-disaster during double Chemistry. Fortunately I am quite swift. I have been a consistent silver medal winner in the one-hundred-metre sprint since mixed infants.

To be honest, before we knew what was really wrong with me I secretly blamed Mum anyway. She'd always had a cleaner coming round to polish the house top to bottom, and kept Airwick anti-tobacco plug-ins set all the way to eleven, even with the windows closed. Because of her my immune system simply wasn't up to coping with the threat of alien bodies. I was practically The Boy In The Bubble; all my autoimmune responses stripped bare by chemical representations of pine forests and summer meadows.

* * *

I had to get the Metro to school that morning because Mum was running late.

'Remember I'm at Jacob's tonight, so if you need me you'll have to ring my mobile,' I called through the living-room doorway.

'Bye, love,' she said and kissed my cheek, handing me a £5 note. 'Get yourself a sandwich at breakfast club. Chris cleared me out last night. He even took the leftover veg.'

School hadn't done breakfast club for over two years by this stage, but it seemed pointless telling Mum as she was always in a hurry in the morning. The extra stress might have tipped her over the edge. Anyway, from the fivers she had been doling out instead of nutrition for the previous two years, I'd saved enough to afford a new laptop and probably still had change for an easyJet flight to Kraków or similar, so I wasn't about to buck that trend.

★　★　★

Jacob wore a thin tie to school and carried around foreign books that he pretended to read on the bus. He thought he had Gallic charm because of his French lineage, but Mum said his family weren't actually French at all, his aunty just ran a caravan site in the Ardèche once but now she bred dogs in Salford with her new husband. I didn't mind so much as Jacob had served as my best friend for over ten years. On his part our friendship stemmed from the fact that I was loyal and amusing and had at least three stories which were guaranteed to entertain, one of which involved a minor local celebrity and was told to me by Chris ages ago. On mine it really was down to the lack of any other option. Jacob was someone I could sit with and look like I was being social and entertaining. Senior school was definitely not *My Moment*. I was wasted in Tyne and Wear, having read at least one book a week since I was in first year.

Until the end of Lower Fifth, though, Jacob would have to do.

*   *   *

'I just want a quick look, to make sure my answers are right,' he said as we walked from the Metro station towards school.

'No.'

'Please?'

'You should have done it yourself.'

Jacob kicked a can on to the road and an old lady swore at him from across the street.

'I did,' he whined.

'Then show me yours and I'll tell you if it's right.'

Jacob always wanted to copy my homework. This was largely because I was quite the intellectual, having achieved all A-Cs in my mock GCSEs.

Jacob was SparkNotes clever at best.

'But you're just so gifted and inspirational. I want to *be* you when I grow up, Frankie,' he said, perhaps not wholly seriously.

'Fine,' I said, and picked up my pace so he was forced to do a skip every third step to keep up with me.

★   ★   ★

After first registration we had General Studies. School had given us our own laptops. They were supposed to be for schoolwork only, but Chris jigged mine about so that I could download music. The plus side being that I had the most extensive music collection of anyone my age, possibly ever. The downside being that it had contracted most major viruses and one or two minor ones, and would perform elaborate and spontaneous emergency reboots halfway through whatever masterpiece I was working on.

The computer warmed up slowly and told me that it was under serious threat and danger. I swore at it and pressed the small orange X at the top right hand of the screen.

We were supposed to be researching the

importance of local government, for a PowerPoint presentation at the end of the week. No one really was, though. Beside me Jacob was watching videos of cats falling off things. And at the other side Gemma Carr was Googling 'Period Two Months Late Cystitis?' with a frantic look in her eyes.

With my screen still open I checked my Homework Diary — or Personal Planner, as we were supposed to call them in Lower Fifth, even though they were just Homework Diaries with sticky labels on the front — to see what delights I'd missed out on the previous night.

It told me that I was analysing three children's stories for English Language using the framework provided for tomorrow's lesson, and planning the *Othello* lunchtime discussion group, which I ran in an attempt to seem like a rounded individual. I had done neither, and just as I was about to start I began feeling funny again. Not sick as such but hazy, like I'd suddenly just woken up there and then, in the middle of a school day, and didn't quite know how to conduct myself. My eyes became more blurry and I could feel my head pounding, so I pushed my chair back and rested my forehead on the desk.

★   ★   ★

I didn't know how long I'd been asleep because when I woke up everyone had left and Miss Spence was standing over me looking concerned.

'You were dead to the world,' she said.

'Ugh,' I said, and stood up quicker than I should have. I felt dizzy and queasy and had to sit back down again.

'Is everything OK, Francis?'

'Yes, Miss,' I said, collecting my things.

'And things are OK at home?'

'Yes. Sorry I fell asleep. It wasn't a comment on the quality of the teaching or anything like that.'

'That's fine. If you ever do need to talk, Francis, you know my door is always open.'

I didn't quite know how to respond to this, so I just nodded and left, feeling stupid.

★ ★ ★

I sat with Jacob in the dinner hall but didn't eat anything because my head was still pounding and even the thought of food was turning my stomach.

'Shall we head off in a minute?' he asked as a commotion started at the far end of the room.

'Suppose,' I said, going to collect my bag. 'I don't think I'm going to make it tonight though, I still feel rough.'

Before Jacob could say anything two first-year girls started shoving one another beside the serving hatch.

'I told you to leave him alone!' the prettier girl, Rameela, shouted in the blonde girl's face while trying to claw out clumps of her hair.

The other girl yelled back as Rameela slammed her to the floor and started dragging her in a horizontal line by her hair. Rameela started to kick out at her but found herself being dragged down too. Soon they just became a blurry mass of fists and flying locks of hair as they writhed on the floor, hammering punches into one another.

The teachers sprang to their feet and began running towards them. The only time our school ever really pulled together as one was in such situations when we formed the Human Barrier, like demonstrators at an anti-war protest. As soon as the teachers stood up and began running towards the eye of the storm, everyone in the dining room pushed their chairs back a foot, so that each adjacent seat at the long rows of tables was touching, creating an impenetrable obstruction which, try as they might, nobody could pass. Eventually they gave up, red in the face and ranting like madmen, and took the long route to the scene of the crime, all the way round the perimeter of the dining tables, by which point the girls were back on the floor, pulling each other's hair.

Mr Thompson was the first to get to them. His fierce grasp on their arms immediately caused them to stop the fight and slump back, panting, glaring daggers at one another.

'You two are so bloody expelled,' he whispered to them as he yanked them through the dining room and out of the door nearest to his office.

*　*　*

As the girls were dragged from view the sounds of the fight were still ringing in my ears. I felt myself become distant from them, as though I was observing my own body from up above, like Peter Pan trying to claw back his own shadow.

'Whoah, you're haemorrhaging!' I heard Jacob say, but couldn't see him any more. My vision became narrower, like a black lens tightening around an image, until there was nothing but darkness.

I went to touch my face and beneath my nose felt warm and damp.

'Oi, dinner lady, brother down!' Jacob yelled from what seemed like a great distance.

I felt myself grow lighter and lighter, until all I remember feeling was the welcome slap of the floor against the side of my face.

'OH MY GOD, HE'S KILLED HIM!' someone shouted as more and more footsteps echoed around my head.

After that it all went dark.

I woke up three hours later in hospital.

★ ★ ★

They took blood samples, which I barely noticed, and also some bone-marrow tests, which weren't quite so easy-going. The spinal tap was not nearly as amusing as the film.

Along the hospital corridor they had a chipped mural of tigers and elephants. In the waiting room there were posters of fundraisers, and photographs of bald kids in headscarves smiling as actors from *Coronation Street* handed over giant cheques with plenty of zeroes.

Mum was silent the whole time. She just stared at the pile of magazines on the table beside us.

I walked over to the vending machine and pressed for a hot chocolate, watching carefully as the jet spat brown dregs all the way to the rim of the cup, and then wincing as the lava-like liquid scalded my fingers through the too-thin plastic. I had no intention of drinking

it; I just wanted something to do. The literature was the same as it had been in every
other waiting room. There were two pam-
phlets on osteoporosis, a doodled-on leaflet
about antibiotics, untouched puzzle books, a
well-thumbed copy of a fishing magazine, and
three back issues of *Woman's Own*. I spent a
moment pitying the unfortunate who met the
NHS's intended demographic, but my sympathies would only stretch so far and eventually
all I had to entertain me was Mum, whose
banter was thin on the ground that day, and
the hot chocolate, whose retrieval had been a
short-lived thrill. So I sat and watched as the
steam moved from thick plumes to sinewy
wisps, and eventually cooled to nothing.

At one point I could see Mum's body
shaking a bit like she had hiccups, even
though I knew she didn't, so I put my hand in
hers. She flinched but didn't look at me. Just
gripped my palm tightly as a fat tear formed
and then rolled down her cheek, taking a dark
line of mascara with it like debris in a
landslide.

'Can we have a takeaway tonight?' I asked.

She told me I could have whatever I liked,
but her voice was hoarse and she had to keep
clearing her throat. I knew how she felt.
Trying not to cry: an art in itself. Once, in
Juniors, Mum let me have some friends

37

round to watch videos. She made popcorn and everything so some of the hardest boys in school came, more for the promised refreshments than the joy of my company. But the whole way through *ET* I had to concentrate on not bursting into tears. When they found him face down in the river, I had to pretend to go to the toilet and sneak into Chris's room so I could wail. Mum says I'm sensitive. Chris says I'm soft. Overall I think I prefer Mum's diagnosis.

★   ★   ★

When we were leaving the hospital Mum went and sat down on a seat beside the main entrance. She still hadn't said anything and neither had I. We were never that chatty in the first place.

She lit a cigarette and put her lighter back in her handbag, where she found a half-eaten bar of chocolate that she handed to me.

I sat chomping and Mum sat smoking, both of us thinking our own thoughts, until the crackling sound of static snapped us back into the moment.

'This is a reminder . . . ' said a man's voice, as if God had finally chosen to reveal Himself, and had done so in a slight Lancastrian twang ' . . . that there is no smoking anywhere on hospital premises. Once again, this is a reminder: there is no smoking allowed anywhere on hospital premises.'

'He'll be lucky,' said Mum, quietly, and carried on puffing away.

I suspect Mum might have been a Punk in her youth.

'We could be fined up to fifty pounds,' I said, pointing to a bright red sign, which stated as much.

'Then we'll flee the country and start new lives in Benidorm,' she said, taking one last drag.

She looked around and found the little camera that they must have been watching us on, then held up the tail end of her cigarette and raised her eyebrows before dropping it into a pot of shrubs.

'Odious little jobsworth,' she said while she hunted through her bag for her keys.

'Will I lose my hair?' I asked in the car.

Mum started the engine and closed her eyes.

'Not now, sweetheart, eh? Let's just keep it together until we get home.'

As she reversed out of the parking space she slid Chris's glum CD into the player and pressed play.

The only person I'd ever known before who had cancer was Miss Patton, our English teacher. During Year Eight she started getting thinner and thinner, and kept nodding off during lessons. Then one day she didn't turn up, and instead we had Mr Bryers who just used to wheel in the big TV and put on a *Romeo and Juliet* video every lesson, the one where if you watch really carefully you can see Olivia Hussey's boob pop out.

None of the teachers ever told us what was wrong. Sometimes they could be crueller than the children. I thought Miss Patton knew this as she never used to eat her lunch in the staff room. She'd just take her sensible sandwiches to her sensible car, and eat them behind the driving seat with the radio playing a sensible lunchtime play inside.

Word got around, though, because Michelle Harman's aunty was a nurse and told Michelle's mum that one of our teachers had been in hospital and hadn't had a single visitor.

For some reason I couldn't stop thinking about her so Jacob and I organised a collection. We got over £16 for a card and a bunch of flowers, only Mr Hall said we weren't allowed the time off to deliver them so Mum had to drive us to the hospital one evening. By the time we got there Miss Patton had been discharged.

She came back for a while, but seemed even more distant than usual. It was as though she'd seen something she couldn't forget, no matter how hard she tried. Then Callum Roberts made a joke about semicolons and she quietly collected her things and never came back. We had two hours to ourselves that day. Or we would have done if Callum hadn't attempted to assassinate David White with a fire extinguisher. Mr Bennett came in to find David curled up on the floor, drowning in a mass of white foam like someone had popped the Michelin Man.

The entire class was put on a month's lunchtime detention so everyone stopped speaking to Callum for nearly a week.

All I could think about was who Miss Patton would tell about her awful day.

* * *

Back home Mum did stick to her word and got us a takeaway, so the day wasn't entirely without perks.

We ate it in silence as neither of us really knew how to behave. It felt like the strange week between Christmas and New Year where something has happened and something is going to happen, but until then all you can do is sit, and wait, and think about it all.

I suppose you do try to imagine things like this happening, but when they do they never pan out the way you expect. When you imagine them there's always music playing in the background, and a camera pans around and catches each emotion on your face as you move from hysterics to terror to verbose 'moments' with your loved ones. But life isn't really like that. Because that would make life a feature-length BBC drama that wins BAFTAs. Real life is quieter, more under-stated. No one is backlit and nothing has a soundtrack and no one has someone cleverer than them writing their lines. And so they just say nothing and get on with it. More's the pity, if you ask me. I quite like the idea of my own soundtrack.

★   ★   ★

Mum hadn't wanted to phone anybody but she did text Chris at some point, though she must have only asked him over for a Chinese because when he arrived it was like nothing was different, which I suppose nothing really was except that it had now been given a name.

'Evening, loved ones,' he said, slumping down straight away on the couch and knocking me out of the way. 'There were two people done on the Metro for heavy petting. How bad is that?' he said, using my fork to pile some leftover noodles on to a plate. 'It was like a porno. The woman . . . and I use the term loosely . . . she had her leg up like this,' he said, chewing a prawn cracker as he reclined on the sofa, 'and the bloke was . . . well . . . you could only really describe it as *rutting*.'

Mum didn't say anything. She just put the cork back into her bottle of wine in an act of unusual restraint. The wheels on our recycling bin would practically buckle beneath the weight of all her empties. After a talk on addiction at school I once did a ten-question quiz on her, pretending it was for homework. The outcome was that she might have been a functioning alcoholic. When I told her this she laughed and said no one had dared accuse her of being functioning before.

Denial is the first of addiction's five stages. The lady who gave the talk at school said so.

'Still rocking the heroin chic vibe, I see?' Chris said to me, and punched my arm playfully. I smiled but didn't say anything. I had lost over two stone and the bags under my eyes had grown six shades darker in hue. I'd measured them against the diagram on the whitening toothpaste box, roughly equating the brown shades there to the purple-green that had started to spread about my eyes.

'What's wrong? Has someone died?' Chris asked.

'*Jesus*,' Mum said, getting up and going into the kitchen with her hand over her mouth.

'What?' Chris said as she left. 'What?' he said again, this time to me. 'That was a prime opening anecdote. Funny, topical, it had everything going for it. I'm wasted on this family,' he said, and turned on the TV.

'I think you should follow Mum.' I nodded towards the kitchen, looking dead mournful. I thought it was a really blunt, poignant thing to say, and Chris would simply know from it that something bad had happened. But *You've Been Framed* destroyed the mood I'd intended to set and Chris just shook his head, giving a big, elaborate moan before pushing a spring roll, whole, into his mouth.

'This better be worth it,' he said, and left me on my own.

★ ★ ★

One of the first things we learn is that people die. Then we start to learn why. Old age is the starting point. It's more or less palatable, something everybody can just about stomach; the Soup of the Day to mortality's grand buffet. People have long and happy lives, we

44

are taught. Then they get tired. Then they just stop, fall asleep, for ever. It's why grand-parents are so useful. For most people our first death is one we always knew was coming. The one we'd been prepared for from day one.

Then we learn more. Guns. War. Disease. Cancer.

The big words. The bad words. The words that never end well.

And now I was one of them. And for a moment on the sofa suddenly that was all I was. That one word printed through me like Blackpool rock. The sound of the TV fell away as I stared down at my own body. The body that had never co-operated. The hair that never stayed moulded into the shape I wanted. The spots that appeared out of nowhere. The small mound of belly that stuck out over the waist of my jeans like I was constantly recovering from Christmas dinner. And those stupid, soft patches of fuzz that sprouted on my face but never fused into the sophisticated five o'clock shadow that I needed to wear so that everybody would know I was a tortured poet.

Then, to top it all off, my body had borne its own would-be killer, and if I died now it would be all that anybody remembered about me. It would be my death that mattered. Not my life. It would be that word. The word that

45

was bigger than me and stronger than me and more famous than I ever would be.

For a second the weight of it seemed so huge that I had to concentrate hard to catch my breath.

Then there were the other, strange things I felt. Excited, a bit. That things were going to change, to become different and focused. And on me, which was a plus. It was like the time Granddad died (which was bad) but I got my first-ever suit, which everyone agreed I wore exceptionally well (which was good.) It was sort of like Yin and Yang, where every white bit has a corresponding black bit, and the black bit has a white bit.

Nothing's ever all bad if you think hard enough about it.

There was also the thought of school. I'd already been told I'd have to miss quite a lot. The doctors had talked about treatment and staying on a special ward and weeks and months and other timescales, which didn't seem to mean anything to me. I didn't like the idea of falling behind in lessons. But on the other hand, the idea of having to re-sit a whole year did hold a certain appeal. To my future classmates in Lower Fifth I would have the wit and wisdom of a village elder or veteran rock star. Girls would flock and boys would flash green with envy. I could hold court and wow them all with tales of my experiences.

I might even consider affecting a cravat.

* * *

By the time they came back in it was like they'd switched bodies. Mum was worryingly upbeat and Chris looked like he'd signed up for Disneyland and got Dunkirk.

He sat down next to me and didn't say a word. Didn't speak. Didn't blink.

'God, this is ridiculous,' Mum said bouncily. 'Come on, let's put a DVD on. Francis love, you pick something,' she continued, popping the cork on her bottle and pouring herself a small glass.

'I don't mind . . .'

'Anything you like, really.'

'I don't. Well, maybe Chris . . .'

'Just pick a bloody DVD, Francis.'

I took the first thing that caught my eye and pressed play.

Everyone sat back and we watched the film. Only no one really watched, we just had an excuse not to look at one another for one hour and twenty-nine minutes precisely, after which I said goodnight and went to bed.

* * *

That night I lay in bed and tried to pinpoint exactly how I felt. I wasn't sure so tried crying, but that didn't work out too well either. I even tried having a deep thought about it all, about what it meant and why and how, only there didn't seem to be anything to think. It just was.

The one thing I did wish was that I had someone to tell; to have a big, heart-breaking scene with, where my quiet bravery would be expressed through their tears and hysterics. In truth there was no one. There was Grandma, I suppose, but she was even tougher than Mum and only cried once at Granddad's funeral, and that was when she realised she'd forgotten the corned beef pie for the wake. And there was Jacob, but he wouldn't get upset because he was emotionally stunted due to the lack of a positive male role model since his dad had been arrested for embezzlement.

My lack of friends had never bothered me before. I'd had other things to occupy my time, like Chris and books and music and plans for the future. It used to worry Mum, though. Once she had me tested for autism, but the tests proved futile. She had asked me why I didn't have any friends except for that idiot with the lank hair (meaning Jacob). I said it was because my real friends would come later. She asked me why I didn't at least try in the meantime, and I told her that I didn't like meeting new people as the ones I did meet I generally didn't like.

I tried to sleep but couldn't and kept tossing and turning, so went back downstairs for a drink. Mum never cried in front of us. Or she never had before. Even with Emma, and when Dad left, if things got too much for her she'd go upstairs and turn on the TV in her room, then come back downstairs five minutes later with red eyes and a fixed grin. She was crying that night, though; crying hard and breathlessly, like she'd been waiting her whole life to cry that way. Chris was holding her tightly to him, as if trying to squeeze her into silence. He looked determined, like he was hatching a plan.

I thought about going inside but didn't know what to say. I felt oddly guilty, so snuck back upstairs before they saw me, and went to bed.

3

When I used to learn big words, I would use them over and over again until eventually they lost their splendour, like a rare coin thumbed so many times it begins to tarnish. I once filled out a feedback form using the word 'superfluous' on six occasions in the Further Comments box, a box which amounted to three dotted lines.

When I realised that 'embellish' was the fancy way of saying 'exaggerate', that was all anyone seemed to do for a while. At Christmas I proudly told Grandma that Mum and I planned on embellishing the tree on the fifteenth and had selected a palette of red and gold embellishments from BHS that year, and that her embellishment of the cake had been dead resplendent (another quality find that month).

It was different when I started learning swear words, particularly when I realised what they meant. I would keep each one secret, like the last bar of chocolate on a doomed voyage, and then when no one else was around I would let it dance and melt on my tongue over and over again. Only this particular routine was cut short when Mrs Lyle from number forty-two went blackberry-picking one day and overheard me muttering a refrain of 'wanker . . . wanker . . . wanker . . . wanker'. She wrote Mum a letter informing her, and posited undiagnosed Tourette's. I was grounded for a week and had the TV taken out of my room.

When they told me I had cancer, the word held a new quality. It felt charged, all potential, guaranteed to cause a reaction. But it was never the same reaction twice, which was a problem. So, for a while, I stopped saying it. I kept it to myself, like a new haircut or a daring pair of trainers, until I felt comfortable letting it loose on the world at large. The word seemed wrong and awkward in my mouth, like the gum-shield I'd once been given as a precursor to the dreaded brace. I would sit on my bed and practise saying it, feeling it catch and snag in my throat, trying to find the right pitch and tone. Painful at first, then becoming easier, more natural, like a splinter making its way from a freshly bathed finger.

Of course, it didn't stay secret for long.

★　★　★

Jacob was quiet when I told him.

'The bad kind or the good kind?' he asked. I didn't entirely know how to respond to this.

51

I knew there were bad and good bacteria, but wasn't aware of the type of cancer that came with benefits. 'No,' he said, trying to explain himself. 'It's just my mum had a cell or something removed once that was a bit dodgy, but she only needed the afternoon off work so it was fine.'

I had deduced that it would take more than an afternoon and a blue plaster to make me better, so eventually settled on the most accurate answer I could come up with.

'Medium, I suppose.'

We settled, eventually, on simply not acknowledging it at all in conversation, unless as a matter of complete medical emergency, which suited me down to the ground.

Not everyone was quite so lax about the situation.

People started taking notice of me where they never had before. Teachers began marking me up on homework even I knew was below par. I was usually a steady B. Not because I was naturally mediocre, but rather I suspect due to the fact that my intelligence was raw and untamed like an artist's or a libertine's. My mind went beyond easy classification; try and pin it down to a standard category and it bucked and writhed, never quite as apparent in black and white as it was in my mind. Also I did a lot of my homework in front of the TV or on the Metro, so my handwriting was sometimes quite hard to read. Either way, my marks were solidly average. After the diagnosis you'd have thought I was one of those pale kids you see on the News who get full marks in every exam they take three years early, only I was achieving such greatness without the inevitable early-twenties breakdown. I didn't mind all that much. I just smiled weakly and whooped inside, each free mark another step to the university of my choice.

Other kids also started to behave strangely to me. No one made eye contact, no one spoke. It was as if for the first time in my life people knew who I was, and chose to demonstrate as much by ignoring me as elaborately as possible.

★   ★   ★

One Wednesday afternoon I was sitting in English Lit when Miss Cartwright came bustling into the classroom and had a word with Mr Bryers.

'Francis Wootton, collect your things. You're being picked up,' he said from the front of the class. I was disappointed because it was getting to the good bit of *Romeo and Juliet*, but I dutifully did as instructed and left with Miss Cartwright.

'It's your appointment,' she said ominously, like we were in some alternate universe where everyone spoke in code.

I told her I didn't have an appointment and she shook her head sadly as she hurried me along the corridor.

'He said you'd say that. That you'd have your days mixed up.'

'He?'

'Never mind, sweetheart. Oh, love, you really are all to hell, aren't you?' she said, turning the corner into the library where the secretaries sorted the registers. 'Off you go, sweetheart, we've told your teachers for this afternoon.'

'But I don't have an appointment . . . '

Miss Cartwright shook her head and dabbed her nose with a handkerchief.

'So brave,' she said, scurrying back behind the counter.

★ ★ ★

Outside I couldn't see anyone and still didn't entirely know what was going on.

'All right, feller?' Chris said eventually, getting out of a car I hadn't seen before.

From inside I could see Fiona waving at me.

54

'What's happening?' I asked.

'Thought we'd have some time together. Nothing heavy. Just a bit of extra-curricular bonding.'

I shrugged and got into the car.

Chris had borrowed it from a friend at work by saying that his little brother was at death's door with cancer (!), but he said it wasn't tempting fate because he knew I'd be fine. He drove like he always does, zigzagging in and out of lanes and leaving a choir of angry toots in his wake.

'We just thought we might as well have some fun,' Fiona explained.

'Don't tell Mum, though,' Chris said as he swerved past a lorry.

'Where are we going?'

'Tyne and Wear is our oyster,' said my brother, and put on a CD.

The drive was the second best bit of the day. None of us knew where we were going. We had no plan. No final destination in mind. We just drove faster and faster until we arrived. And when we did all I could think about was how much fun it had been getting there.

'Your uniform's looking especially avant-garde today,' said Fiona as we pulled into the parking space at the beach.

'Thanks. The trousers are actually skinny

jeans, look!' I held up my thigh to show her the discreet denim, which was forbidden at school. The jeans weren't actually supposed to be skinny. That was just a lucky coincidence. None of my clothes fitted properly because I was too scared to try anything on. I once got stuck in a pair of pants in Topman and started hyperventilating. Mum must have heard me panting and groaning and assumed I was doing something ungodly, because she threw the dressing-room curtains open with a mortified look in her eyes and then burst into hysterics when she saw me struggling. She had never been very good in a crisis and provided little in the way of emotional stability. It was a wonder I turned out as stoical as I did. Things took an even worse turn when she started trying to yank them off my calves. The salesgirls just stood in the corner asking if we needed any help and Mum made a joke about them having to fetch the Jaws of Life, which was a) not funny, and b) inappropriate given my shortness of breath at the time. I could easily have blacked out through stress.

The memory of it still haunted me; the upshot being I had clothes which either hung loose and baggy around me or were so skin-tight I could barely move. The jeans fell into the latter category.

' . . . and I put black braces on underneath my blazer.' I dipped my shoulder to provide supporting evidence. 'It's a nod to Patti Smith on the cover of *Horses*. No one got it, though. I don't think the rest of Lower Fifth are too well versed in seventies counterculture.'

'More's the pity,' she said, and put her arm around me. 'Do you know something, Francis?' She took a long sip of Tizer and continued, 'Years from now there are going to be women crying on their hen nights, telling their friends that you were the best they ever had.'

'Not at the rate I'm going,' I said flatly.

It was true. I'd only ever kissed two girls, and one of them was my second cousin for a dare when I was six. The other was Paula Amstel who wore a corrective shoe and couldn't say her Rs properly.

'Oh, Francis, it'll happen,' Fiona assured me.

'Do you think the Make a Wish Foundation could sort something out . . . you know, all things considered?' I asked, only half seriously.

Chris laughed from the front of the car and impressively managed to span three parking spaces before stopping the engine.

'I'll get a ticket, Don Juan,' he said, still

chuckling, and slammed the door behind him.

When he was gone Fiona gave me a funny look. Not embarrassed, the way everyone at school had started to look, or pityingly, like the teachers did. She looked like she was on a mission and determined to succeed.

'Francis,' she said, glancing through the back window like she was scared someone might be spying on us, 'I'm going to do something now and I need you to know it's an act of humanitarian goodwill, OK?'

I nodded.

'I mean it! I don't want to be put on some register.'

'OK.'

She sighed again and sat up straight in her seat.

'You can look but you can't touch, deal?'

'Deal,' I said.

Before I knew it she had lifted her sweater up and pulled down her bra.

I sat there, stunned.

I can categorically confirm that they were even better than Juliet's.

'There,' said Fiona, pulling her top down. 'And if anyone asks, you can say we did tops and fingers. I'll back you up that far. Beyond that you're on your own.'

I nodded even though I wasn't entirely sure

what she meant. I wasn't very good at sex, even in theory. This was probably down to the fact that I had no real friends except for Jacob, and his track record with the opposite sex was as lousy as mine. Sex education was a joke because they only ever put on scratchy videos of women in labour and cartoons of men in white shorts swimming towards giant orbs. And even though she'd tried, Mum's attempt at The Talk hadn't been entirely illuminating. She just sat on my bed one day, stroking the sheets absent-mindedly, and eventually asked if I knew that people got off with one another. When I told her I did she looked relieved and said, 'Good, well, if you need any gaps filling in then we've got broadband and I never check the history . . . ' Then left to make tea.

* * *

The three of us walked along the promenade for a while and chatted about music and films. Chris kept stopping to text me the names of bands he said I should listen to and fall in love with, and Fiona kept linking my arm each time we passed groups of kids bunking off from school, making it look like she was my girlfriend.

About half an hour later we passed an

ice-cream van, which looked sad and lonely in the winter sun, and Fiona dashed across for some emergency supplies. I hung around to wait for her but Chris said she'd catch us up and led me to a seat overlooking the water.

We sat quietly together for a while. Fiona had the knack of luring into conversation just about anyone she talked to. Even Grandma would talk to her for hours despite the fact that Fiona had tattoos and often wore clothes that exposed her navel. But something told me that this was more choreographed than her usual social detours.

Chris and I sat and watched two gulls fighting over a greasy sheet of newspaper, and I closed my eyes as the damp sea fret passed across my face. My brother didn't speak, just prodded the toe of his Converse into a puddle on the ground.

'Chris,' I said eventually, worrying about how long Fiona would be able to tolerate the conversation of the ice-cream man, 'do you want to have a poignant conversation?'

He laughed and shrugged, kicking a fag end from the puddle so that it slid off the edge of the promenade.

'Dunno. Do you?'

'Not really. Can't things just be normal?'

'Not really,' he said, and laughed again,

only more sadly this time. 'I'm so sorry, Frankie,' he continued, rubbing a hand across his mouth.

'There's nothing for you to be sorry about. It just is, I suppose. Besides they're going to do loads to get rid of it.'

'Yeah, I know,' he said, 'it'll be over before you know it. And I'll feel like a right tit about busting you out of school and forcing you into a Deep and Meaningful.'

'Probably. I'm glad you got me out of school, though. I'd forgotten my copy of *Birdsong*.'

'Are you scared?' he asked.

'Not really. I know the bits I need off by heart.'

Chris bumped his shoulder against mine. He had gone to the trouble of securing an automobile, so the least I could do was meet him halfway on the big emotional scene he'd obviously envisioned.

'I suppose so,' I said after a while. 'It just feels so big. Too big. It's like . . . remember that summer when Mum had the swimming pool built in the back garden without measuring it properly first?' I asked, and Chris laughed at the memory of one of her more obscure tangents. 'And how, until she got the builders to take it out again, we had to walk around it with our backs against the fence just to get our bikes out of the shed? It's like that. Like suddenly it's right there, with no planning, no warning. And you can't *not* notice it. It's in the middle of everything, and it's ruining everything, but nobody knows how to get around it. I think I just want someone to tell us how to make it work, you know, how to make it fit in with everything else. Because it doesn't feel like there's enough room for it. I've got GCSEs to think about for a start.'

Chris laughed and put his arm around me.

'What we need is an idiot's guide to leukaemia. Maybe Waterstone's will have something in.'

I felt all the hairs on my arms stand up. I did not like Chris saying the word. No matter how gentle they made their voices or how low they forced their tone, other people saying it made it sound like an accusation.

'Yeah, exactly,' I said after a while. 'That'd make everything fine, if we just knew how it was all going to pan out. A timescale. That's what we need. Maybe a wall chart, like my revision timetable.'

We both laughed, and Chris pulled his arm tighter around me.

'There isn't anything I wouldn't do to swap places with you, Frankie.'

'I know.'

'There isn't anything I won't do to make it easier for you.'

'I don't think there's anything you can do.'

'I know,' he said. 'But I'll try.'

We were quiet again and eventually I told him that there was one thing he could help me with.

'And I need you to answer me honestly.'

'I will.'

'I just need to know. I mean, I probably do already know, but I just need you to explain exactly . . . '

'What?'

'I mean, obviously I *know*, but just, if you could tell me for definite . . . '

'What is it, Frankie?' he said, looking nervy. 'Just say.'

'Well, I suppose, what I mean is . . . what exactly do people mean by tops and fingers?'

★   ★   ★

We got chips because the smell from the shop made our mouths water, and then didn't eat them because they seemed so much more exciting in theory than in practice. We just sat in a bus stop because it had started to drizzle, warming our hands on the soggy newspaper, and chatted about all kinds of unimportant things, as if nothing was different, just like it was any other day when Chris and Fiona had kidnapped me from school. At one point I thought I saw Mum's car and started to have difficulty breathing when I thought my cover might be blown, but Fiona said cancer was like a dozen get-out-of-jail-free cards: no one was going to pull me on anything behavioural for some time to come. Not even Mum.

They dropped me at the far end of the street so as not to arouse suspicion, and then ruined the whole operation by tooting six loud bursts of the horn as they drove away. I panicked and threw myself into Mrs Jackson's privet hedge. Truancy can result in a fine, which Mum could probably afford but which would also besmirch the otherwise immaculate permanent record I needed for applying to university.

When I got in the house was quiet. Usually Mum had on music or the TV. Sometimes both. She was not like me. I needed an almost Zen-like state of calm when I did homework, and my desk had to be organised in a way that meant everything was both symmetrical and ordered by size. Mum's desk usually looked like a bomb had gone off, and her paperwork was always dog-eared and with coffee stains. It was a wonder she'd come as far as she had in life. To me, presentation was key. That was why I even had her iron my boxer shorts.

Grandma's shopping trolley was in the

hallway so I knew she must be visiting. This usually meant good things, primarily a pound pocket money and probably some sweets also. Grandma's company itself varied in quality. Sometimes she could be a real laugh. She and I were allies. When Grandma was about I was never to blame.

Other times she just made clucking sounds at everything Mum seemed to do, and Mum huffed and puffed like a teenager until she finally started yelling about stuff that happened ages ago and it all kicked off big style. The atmosphere sometimes became too much for me to take, so I removed myself to watch *The Simpsons* on the TV in the conservatory. That was my sanctuary. It was like the cluttered study of some Victorian detective. I'd had many of my most profound thoughts in here. I think it might have been because of the combination of the endless view towards the sea and the muggy atmosphere, which lent the place the atmosphere of an opium den or Roman steam bath.

There was no sound coming from the front room until I made it inside. I saw Grandma sitting next to Mum on the sofa. She had her hand resting in Mum's lap. This was the first sign something was wrong. The TV had been muted. Another bad sign.

When I arrived inside Mum stood up and I

65

could see that she had been crying again. I assumed that the full implication of my illness must finally have hit her and she was struggling to cope so I moved towards her to comfort her, only she reached out and slapped me across the face. It wasn't hard. If anything, the sound was louder than the sting. But the point was made. Grandma held her hand to her mouth in shock, the way ladies of her age do. I was surprised she didn't flutter her handkerchief and slide unconscious to the floor. She was, after all, witness to the birth of abuse in the family home.

'They told me you were at the hospital,' Mum said, starting to cry. My cheek began to sting and I was cross that she was the one who was going to be getting all the sympathy. I thought about forcing myself to cry but it was no good. I could not bring myself to whore my emotions that way. So I just stood there, dumbstruck.

'You stupid, stupid boy,' Mum said, pulling me towards her. 'Don't ever do that again.'

She hugged me for a moment and, though reluctant at first, I eventually relented and hugged her back. Mum heaved wet sobs on to my shoulder. I knew she'd be able to smell the sea on my clothes. I also started to panic that she'd smell Fiona's cigarettes on my uniform and assume I'd been smoking. If skipping three lessons warranted a facial assault then the Lord knew what smoking might induce. It would probably be enough to inspire an entire trilogy of memoirs. Talk show hosts would end up congratulating me on my Journey.

But Mum didn't seem to notice the smoke so I carried on hugging her. I was surprised she'd got in touch with the school in the first place, or vice versa. They'd never seemed to communicate that much in the past. One parents' evening Mum sat for forty minutes in the hallway of Infants before remembering I'd moved up into Secondary, then came back and blamed me for never showing her the letters I'd brought home.

I peeked over her shoulder to try and see whether or not I was in time for *The Simpsons*, but she must have misinterpreted my curiosity for affection because she started hugging me tighter, saying how sorry she was and how I was never to frighten her like that again. Grandma gave me a look and nodded, which meant she was proud of me, and suddenly I was proud of myself too. In that moment I was keeping my entire family afloat, and safe from complete emotional breakdown.

I suddenly felt quite burdened.

Tea was a sombre affair. Grandma told us stories about Granddad, which I'd heard a thousand times before but still smiled at because I liked hearing her tell them. Grandma was different when she talked about Granddad. It was as if someone jiggled her aerial and suddenly the picture became that bit clearer. Mum loved hearing about him too. They were always close. Mum had him and Grandma living with us when he had been unwell, and took loads of time off work to help out. Even Grandma said she'd made her proud, the way she had behaved.

Grandma was still there when I went to bed. When I hugged her to say goodnight she drew me tightly to her and gave me a surprisingly wet kiss and whispered in my ear that she loved me. I said it back, then said goodnight to Mum before making my way to bed.

The day's downward spiral had left me feeling low. I logged on to eBay to check my positive feedback comments in the vain hope that it might give me a confidence boost. It did, slightly, but not as much as usual. So I started searching for songs that spoke to the mood of the day. I came up with a promising opening trio: 'Life on Mars' by David Bowie,

'She's Leaving Home' by the Beatles, 'Fast Car' by Tracy Chapman.

I was starting to become engrossed in the task when I heard a knock at the bedroom door and Mum asked if she could come in.

I had to think twice before granting her access, fearing another outbreak of violence. Eventually I closed the laptop as quietly as I could and put it on the floor beside the bed, lying back as though I had just been woken up. I said that she could, but used a weak, tired voice so that she'd know to be gentle.

When she came in she started fussing about my desk, putting used tissues in the bin and pretending to be dead interested in the homework I'd left open to prove it was actually being done.

'I know you weren't asleep,' she said, sitting on my bed. 'I could hear you closing the laptop.'

From downstairs I could hear the *Coronation Street* theme tune playing, which meant it was ten o'clock and Grandma was catching up with the repeat.

'Sorry I skived,' I said. I wasn't really sorry, I was pleased I'd had the day to myself. I wasn't even that sorry for scaring Mum any more, not after her outburst. But I said it anyway, to try and make her feel better.

'That's OK. Sorry I went off on one. It

wasn't my finest moment.'

I shrugged. I was not quite ready to accept my mother's apology. She needed to know that this sort of behaviour could not be condoned. To normalise it would only encourage a repeat performance.

'Oh, Francis, what are we going to do, eh?' she said eventually.

I told her that I'd go to school every day from now on, even weekends if she wanted me to, and never bunk off again. She just wafted her hand and took a sip of water from my cup beside the bed.

'That's fine. It's over and done with. I mean . . . this has blown a hole right through me Francis, you know? And I feel like I shouldn't say that because the last thing you should be doing right now is worrying about me.'

She was right. My energies were best reserved for the battle ahead. I didn't say as much, though, just nodded sympathetically.

'I'm not very good at all this,' she said, teasing the feathers of my dream catcher. 'I can cope, just about, in my own way. But I don't know what you need me to be. That's my problem.'

'You've always managed before.'

'Well, before was different. I'm having a bit of a crisis of confidence here, Frankie. Good timing, eh?' she said, and laughed. 'I suppose all I'm saying, Francis, is that whatever it takes, I'm going to get you through this. And I'm going to be whatever you need me to be, whenever you need me to be it. I just want you to talk to me. Not to close up. Not to go inside yourself and save it all for the blog or for Chris or for that cretin you knock about with. Just let me know, Francis. Everything I do is for you. It might not always seem that way but it is. So, that's it really, love. Just let me know what you need, and I'll be it.'

I nodded and went to hug her because suddenly I had forgiven her, and felt awful for scaring her, and just wanted to show her that she was always what I needed her to be, even when she was going off on one.

When she hugged me back she felt weaker than she ever had before. Normally when she hugs me it's the way she shakes hands with men at work, determined and solid, like she's proving a point. This time she just sort of sank into me, like she had finished a marathon and I was wrapping her in a foil blanket.

'Goodnight, love. No more internet tonight,' she said. 'Try and get some sleep.'

She turned off my lamp and closed the door behind her. I waited until I heard the creak of the last stair before I picked up my laptop and carried on making my playlist.

4

'In the face?' Chris said, genuinely shocked. I hadn't intended to say anything, but once he had arrived and we were alone I thought I had better address the issue, just so he knew where we were at as a family.

'Yeah, but not hard. At first I was angry and thought about pressing charges, maybe even divorcing myself from her, like a Culkin or something.'

'Maybe you should have.'

'It's OK. I've forgiven her now. I just think it's all a bit much for her. She's doing really well, mostly . . . She's all right.'

'She's the sort of woman they name hurricanes after,' said Fiona. She was kneeling on the kitchen bench, stretching her arm to the very back of the food cupboard. Mum had taken Grandma out shopping and told Chris he had to come and spend some time with me. The second the car had left the drive Fiona turned up with an empty carrier bag and she and Chris began swarming the supplies.

'She's started hiding the good stuff at the back, behind the flour and stuff. Just dig deep,' Chris said, opening the fridge and fleecing a tub of Utterly Butterly and two packets of Cheestrings.

'Don't tell her I told you,' I warned him.

'I think we'd better call it a day,' Fiona said, pulling out a family-sized carton of stir-in pasta sauce before closing the cupboards. 'Little and often . . . that way she's none the wiser. She'll just think Punchbag's got his appetite back.'

'Spoken like a master criminal,' Chris said, sealing up the bag. 'Oh, one more thing.' He opened the freezer and took out a packet of chicken breasts and two bags of chilli Mum had frozen for emergency mid-week teas. 'For protein,' he said to me, half apologetically.

Fiona grabbed the bag and ruffled my hair before fleeing the scene of the crime. We heard her shut the door behind her and we were alone.

'Do you want to watch a film or something?' Chris asked.

'In a bit,' I said, texting Mum to say we needed butter. I didn't want him to starve but even I wouldn't tolerate dry toast on his behalf. She texted straight back, asking me to relay to Chris that he was to stop foraging in her cupboards, and that Fiona was to vacate the premises and perhaps ask her own mother for food donations. I will not recite what she said word for word due to my modesty and discretion.

By the time Mum got back from shopping it was the in-between hours, when it's too late for lunch and too early for tea.

'Just have a biscuit or something,' she said when I moaned that I was hungry. It seemed cancer was not like having a cold, where everything was brought to you on a tray in bed. Because I was coping so admirably, Mum's sympathies only stretched so far. Not so far as an afternoon sandwich, apparently.

★   ★   ★

Later that afternoon Jacob visited for a bit and brought me a present.

'They're from Mum, for when you go in,' he said.

That was the other reason Mum had made Chris come round. It was Sunday. On Monday I was moving on to the specialist unit to start treatment. I had been trying not to think about it. For some reason the thought of trying to get better seemed scarier than everything that had gone before.

The present was a pair of striped pyjamas, which seemed like a bleak reminder to someone in my position, but I thanked him anyway.

There was also a Get Well Soon card with a £5 W. H. Smith voucher inside.

I showed Mum the presents and she said it was very kind of Jacob's mum. She likes her even less than she likes Jacob, thanks to an incident at our Infant school's bake sale. Mum had bashed about some shop-bought cakes and sent them in for me to sell. Jacob's mum had pointed out that they were on special offer at Sainsbury's that week, and when Mum found out she went off it.

Mum is good at grudges.

I told her I thought the £5 voucher would perhaps pay for writing supplies — maybe a notepad and a fountain pen — that I could use to document the coming months, but Mum said I'd be lucky if a fiver would get me a carrier bag in Smith's these days, and that if I wanted a jotter and biro she'd buy them for me. After some bartering we came to an agreement whereby I would give her the voucher, so that it would afford her a magazine or similar, and in turn she would buy me whatever I wanted from Smith's. Usually she's far harder to bargain down.

'He's not stopping for tea, is he?' Mum had asked at the top of her voice when I'd gone into the kitchen to get Jacob some pop. I said no and she said, 'Good, it's a family meal tonight, so he can't stay long.'

75

It suited me down to the ground. We'd played a computer game even though I never really knew what I was doing with them. Mum had been given it free by one of the people she worked for, and handed it down to me in the hope I might find a hobby that was normal for someone my age. All I ever really used it for was to fill in the silences when Jacob came round, of which there were many that day.

'You scared?' he asked at one point.

People kept asking me this. The stupidity of the question never seemed to dawn on them. There could be only two answers. Either the answer was no, in which case there was no point in talking about it. Or it was yes, in which case I certainly wouldn't want to talk about it. Plus nobody really wanted to know. If I'd opened my mouth and told Jacob how I really felt at that point, he'd have bolted. He was going through the motions and I hated him for it.

'No,' I said, lying.

At first it had all seemed slightly exotic, like a foreign neighbour or a famous family member. The words being thrown about were ones I only knew from films or TV. But the closer it came to moving on to the unit, the closer I came to wanting to burst into tears at every given opportunity. Treatment could only go two ways, I kept thinking. Nothing said it would go the right one. It didn't help that luck hadn't been entirely on my side of late.

'I wouldn't be either,' Jacob said, shooting me in the face with a machine gun.

I paused the game and told him he had to leave because Mum was starting tea.

'But I was winning,' he said.

He was not. I was luring him into a false sense of security. That he'd fallen for it was proof of my prowess.

'Well, you've got to go, Mum says. Tea's nearly ready. Thanks for coming round, though.'

'Fine,' he said, and got up to leave. 'I hope you're OK. Do you want me to come and visit?'

The responsibility of deciding was something I could have done without so I just shrugged.

'If you like,' I said.

I let Chris see him out.

★ ★ ★

I had three visitors in quick succession while I was packing my things that night, like Scrooge in *The Muppet Christmas Carol*. The hospital had provided a list of suggested items (pyjamas, slippers, toothbrush) but I had second-guessed them and begun thinking outside the box. I was looking for my smartest shirt to pack so that I was prepared in case I received any special visitors — like a passing princess with a TV crew in tow, eager to touch the lame — when Chris came in and said he was proud of me, even though I hadn't done anything to warrant that. He gave me a mix CD, which he said would help when I was feeling down. I thought it might have been an inspirational message album. I'd bought something similar from a garden centre once when my SATs were giving me sleepless nights. It hadn't worked. But Chris said it was a failsafe power drive of the most energising rock songs he could think of. He told me I'd be fine, and also gave me a £50 top-up voucher and said if I ever needed him I should ring, no matter what time of the day or night it was.

Then Grandma came in and hobbled over to my bed, sitting down right on top of the three T-shirts I had folded as perfectly as any shop assistant might. She asked me if I had enjoyed dinner. I said I had, but was beginning to worry about Mum's heavy hand with the salt shaker. Sodium can lead to high blood pressure, heart failure, and death. We had recently watched a documentary about it in Food Tech. Grandma shook her head and said it'd do me no harm; that life was for living. She said Granddad lived eighty-three years on a diet of salt and pastry, and that a piece of fruit had never passed his lips. I told her this was more than likely down to luck. Then she went all quiet and said she was proud of me too. By this point the whole process was becoming wearing. She took my hand and made me sit down close to her so I could feel her bony frame beneath her clothes. With a shaky hand she snuck something out of her side pocket and handed it to me.

'It was your Granddad's,' she said.

It was a small silver pendant on which there was the outline of a man holding a stick.

'St Christopher,' she said, proudly. 'It's not real silver, but no one'll know if you don't tell them. Supposed to keep you safe when you're travelling. Your granddad never took it off.'

I did not have the heart to remind her that the heart attack that would eventually kill Granddad got into full swing in the ambulance, as it zoomed past Bargain Booze.

'Oh, love,' she said, hoisting herself up from the bed, using my shoulder for support. 'You just watch how you go, flower, you're for ever in my prayers.'

She gave me a big kiss and then left.

By this time I was massively behind with my packing. Added to which my T-shirts all had to be refolded, thanks to Grandma's utter disregard for her surroundings.

Mum came in last and was quiet again.

'Do you want any help with your packing?' she asked.

I told her no, because I had drafted a plan of my suitcase accounting for every inch of space.

'Well, in that case, can I just sit here?'

I said yes. Mum was not given to asking permission of anyone. I thought that denying her my company might lead to further hysterics so carried on with my task as she sat toying with an action figure that had escaped the clutter cull of the preceding spring.

'You'll be fine, you know,' she said. 'If there's anything you want to talk about, Francis, ever, I'm here.'

I stopped folding my third best pair of boxers and jammed them in the case.

'I know,' I said, but could feel my voice wobbling and my throat getting tighter. 'I don't know why everyone keeps telling me things I know. I'm clever enough to realise them for myself. I got nearly all sevens on my SATs and I'm predicted all A to Cs on my GCSEs, which you'd know if you ever read my reports. I understand everything — ' Now my eyes were watering and my throat scratched with each syllable. 'I just wish people would stop treating me like I was stupid and let me get on with my packing!' I said, and knocked the case to the floor.

Mum looked shocked. I am renowned as the pacifist within the family. Conflict is normally beyond me.

She went to pick up the case then thought better of it. Instead she just grabbed me and held me tight against her. At first I tried to fight her off, but resistance was futile.

I sat down on the bed, crying hard into her shoulder, and she lay back. I felt my face get redder and redder. I was choking on tears. Each time I tried to say something they washed over the words like the tide round a drowning man.

I must have nodded off sometime soon after, because when I woke up it was morning and I was in bed. My case had been packed too, and even I had to admit Mum had done an all right job of it.

★   ★   ★

The teenage unit was not like other parts of the hospital. For a start there was a chill-out room attached, which looked like the sort of thing housemates were rewarded with on *Big Brother*. It had a TV the size of a small car, and every games console that ever existed. There was even a drinks machine and two comfy sofas. They looked out of place in a hospital setting, like the relative who turns up to a funeral in a tracksuit. Also everyone there was a little bit more cheery than anywhere else, which I found immediately suspicious given the circumstances.

'Hiya, darling, you find us all right out in the west wing?' Jackie said when Mum and I made our way inside. The ward was at the farthest edge of the hospital, practically in a different postcode. I'd had to sit down once on the way in because I was feeling shaky and out of breath. Mum refused my request for a wheelchair. She was always more stick than carrot.

Jackie probably had some fancy job title but she was essentially head of the nursing team. She said everyone on the ward answered to her, and that if I stuck with her she'd see me right. Everyone there treated you like a paying guest and made sure to use your name at least twice in any conversation. They didn't remember it because they liked you. It was conveniently printed out on a laminated sheet at the foot of the bed.

'Traffic was a nightmare but we got here in

the end,' Mum said. She was normally much sharper than that. It seemed small talk was the first thing to suffer under stress.

'Nowt worse. Do you want something to eat, flower? Lunch isn't for a while yet but I could scavenge you some toast?' Jackie asked me.

I said I did not, and started unpacking on the bed that we had been shown to on arrival.

'Well, I'll let you get settled in and be along shortly to see how you're getting on,' she said, and left us to it.

Another thing that grated on me was that the atmosphere on the ward seemed worryingly informal. Everyone, except for the occasional doctor, introduced themself by their first name. I did not appreciate this touch. It was the same at school. In Sixth Form apparently you got to call teachers by their first names. This thought had already caused me some anguish. Sue is not someone who once caught me looking at the rude bits of *Sons and Lovers* and sent me out for not paying attention to the lesson; Mrs Bancroft is. The whole situation in the unit made me uneasy and caused me to question the legitimacy of my carers' credentials. Marc had muscles and a tattoo that poked out beneath one sleeve of his tunic. I assumed he was given his job as part of some sort of rehabilitation scheme. He was interested in football and dance music and kept trying to talk to me about girls. I suspect he was what they call a reformed character. I guessed that all sorts of unpleasantness lurked in his backstory.

Amy was not, actually, called Amy. Her real name was Thai and too difficult to pronounce for most people there. I told her that whenever I went to a foreign country I made an effort to learn the language, but 'Amy' seemed shy and then a bit cross when I kept asking her for her real name, so I eventually dropped the subject. I made it my mission to find out, though. It did not seem fair that her heritage should have to be erased to suit the idiot patrons of the NHS.

At first there were only three of us on the unit. I lay on one side of the room, in my bed, with a curtain that could be pulled at my discretion but which they suggested I kept open. I often ignored this advice. I craved solitude so that I could contemplate and stuff. Next to me was an empty cot waiting ominously to be filled. Across the room there were two other beds. Kelly occupied the one closest to the window that didn't open. Next to her lay Paul.

He spoke sometimes but not all that often. I knew his sort. I was quite good at reading people, being one of life's natural observers. Chris came in handy for filling in the bigger gaps in my knowledge — for example, the fact that Lindsey Buckingham was the boy in Fleetwood Mac and Stevie Nicks the girl — but at a grassroots level I am perfectly capable of analysing both individual characters and, in turn, whole sub-sections of society.

E.g. if we were all in *The Breakfast Club*, Paul would have been the Emilio Estevez character. He was sporty and good-looking in an obvious way. He had loads of friends and, despite a noticeable lack of visitors, was keen to remind us of this fact.

He behaved the way all boys like him behave around the sort of people they wouldn't usually associate with. He was pleasant and talked sometimes, but stayed for ever at arm's length lest I get the wrong idea and wander up to him in JD Sports one day while he was in town with his crew, destroying his whole life in the process.

But I knew all about boys like Paul. He had to be nice to me at the moment because he had to be surrounded by people. This was because boys like him were, essentially, pasta. Everyone thought they loved him because they had never been forced to experience the true blandness of him on his own. Paul was surface all the way to the bone.

Kelly was equally cookie cutter, even if she didn't sit as comfortably into my Breakfast Club analogy. Socially she was from the same tribe as Paul. They didn't go to the same school, but they might as well have done. She wore make-up even though she spent all of her time in bed, did not intend to further her education, and spent most of her time before she was in the unit in supermarket car parks with boys who drove loud cars.

It was a triumph of geography that she and Paul never shared a pregnancy scare.

★   ★   ★

For a while it was just us three. We'd chat, at times. But the Venn diagram of our interests seldom overlapped, so by and large I was without allies. One morning, not long after I'd arrived, I tried putting my Breakfast Club analogy to them. I explained the theory of *mise-en-scène*, which I'd read about in an A-level Media Studies textbook. The theory is that everything in the frame is significant. So you can pause a film and see the red in the background as a sign of bad things to come, or the cigarette hanging from the woman's lips as a suggestion of a wild, careless streak in her character.

I began to explain that the *mise-en-scène* of this unit was quite apt to the dynamics of our relationship. Only as I was moving fluidly on to my second point Paul pretended to fall asleep. I carried on anyway, and assumed he was taking it all in with his eyes shut. But then Kelly rolled her eyes and told me to shut up and stop being gay (she could be quite coarse).

Then Paul more than gave himself away as a faker by snorting a laugh before giving Kelly a quick glance and closing his eyes again while he fiddled with the volume on his iPod.

It was at this point that I decided not only was their sense of superiority inflated, but I was to face my long and arduous journey alone. I recorded this conclusion in my Diary of Observations.

★ ★ ★

Mum stayed as long as she could on the first day. She kept rearranging the photographs and books I had lined up in perfect symmetry on the bedside locker, and I told her I wished she'd stop. There was method to their arrangement. The books I wanted people to think I read I had placed on top of the pile. The books I was supposed to read were lodged directly beneath, in an effort to shame me into attempting them. The books I would actually read I had placed at the bottom to try to curb the likelihood of my picking them up first.

'Would they not be better off in the drawer? Just taken out one at a time?' Mum kept asking.

I said not as I tried to work out the controls for my bed.

'Oh, God, I think it's broken!' I yelled as I pressed the wrong button and the whole structure started vibrating beneath me, rippling like a lilo in a swimming pool.

'Give it here,' Mum said, pressing a button that made my legs start to levitate slowly.

Across the room I could see Kelly and Paul trying not to laugh just as Mum found the right switch and the bed began to crank back into its correct alignment.

'Daft sod,' Mum said, putting the control back in its holster.

Soon after both Kelly's and Paul's family came to visit and I could tell Mum was paying attention to what they were saying, trying to gauge just how bad things might get, or perhaps even scoring herself against their ability to cope.

They all said hello as they came in and Mum was especially polite. I wasn't in the mood to entertain so I started pulling my blanket up over my legs, hoping they would take the hint that I was unwell and needed a peaceful environment. It was still afternoon, not nearly dark, but there was only one seat so it made sense to let Mum have that and for me to get acquainted with my temporary nest for the next few weeks.

At one point Kelly's mother smiled across at us and Mum gave her a nod.

'I'm sure I used to know her,' she whispered to me. Kelly's mum pulled the curtain around her daughter's bed and began whispering, and then it sounded like someone was crying. I saw Mum shudder and then carry on like nothing had happened.

'I'll put your Lucozade in the bottom drawer, and Grandma sent some grapes along but I left them in the house because they were on the turn. I packed you some multivitamins instead.'

'It's all right, you can go,' I said. 'I know you'll be back tomorrow, but you will have to leave me here eventually.'

Mum went quiet and her head drooped.

'I know,' she said finally, bending down and kissing my forehead. 'Do you want me to leave you to get settled in, make friends with your little roommates?'

'I'll probably just read,' I said. Then saw

her shake her head and added, 'But I will try.'

'You're a good lad,' she said, giving me a hug, 'a good, brave lad.'

She kissed me again and reminded me that her phone would be on all night, and that if I needed anything I was to call her straight away.

She said she'd be back tomorrow, and told me to take care. Then she was gone. I saw her walk slowly out of the ward, nodding to Paul's family as she passed them. The windows looking on to the ward were frosted and had a thin metal mesh. As Mum turned to walk away behind them I saw her blur and fade into a ghost of her own shape. Then I saw her stop in her tracks, and Jackie must have seen her too because the next thing I saw was her giving Mum a hug and leading her out towards the nurses' station.

5

Amber arrived on the fourth day, and from then on everything changed for me.

Paul had been sick for two nights in a row. It was like a conspiracy. Throughout the day he would just sit quietly, wincing whenever he moved and the tube he'd had inserted in his nose snagged on his nostril. Then at night it sounded like a pack of rabid dogs had taken up residence in his bed. Marc kept coming in to help him, but all night I could hear retching and the sound of liquids being sloshed about. Every once in a while it would seem like he'd settled. Then, just as I could feel myself nodding back to sleep, it would start again.

'You're all right. See it up, lad,' I could hear Marc whisper as Paul groaned some more.

'Sleep is vital to recovery,' I told Mum. 'If I can't sleep then the whole thing is pointless. Can't I get a private room? I think I'd handle this much better on my own.'

'Nice to see your old spirit's intact,' Grandma said, chewing on one of the grapes she had brought for me, which she had monopolised and didn't seem to be in the mood to share.

'Fiona sent you this,' Chris said, pulling out a copy of *FHM*. She'd Sellotaped a photograph of herself, giving two thumbs up, on to the model's face. 'She says she'll come and visit you as soon as she's back from her shoot in Milan.'

'I think she could be a model,' I said.

'*You don't say?*'

Mum took the magazine and tucked it into the farthest corner of the drawer.

'Some things never change . . . *sadly*,' she said, and poured herself a glass of Lucozade. I cleared my throat and nodded towards the level in the bottle.

'Bloody hell, Francis, I'll buy you a crate of the stuff if you want. Anyway it hasn't been touched since I was last here.'

That was not the point.

'Oh,' she said, pulling something from her bag, 'this came from school.'

It was a card with two dozen names and get well messages scrawled inside. On the front was a picture of a teddy bear with a bandage on its head.

'Bonny, eh? Is that from your little friends?' Grandma asked, taking the card and inspecting the photograph on the front.

'Ooh,' she said, handing it back to Mum. 'They left the price on.'

'Do you want me to put it up?' Mum asked.

'No,' I said. The picture was crass and juvenile, and would have been at odds with the impressive array of literature I had on display. It would ruin my reputation as the ward's sophisticate.

'Fine. I'll put it in the drawer with the porno and the iPod. How you getting on, *you know?*'

Mum whispered something in my ear, nodding to the beds across from us where Paul and Kelly were pretending not to listen.

I shrugged.

'OK, I suppose. I think I'm misunderstood, though, like Van Gogh was.'

Grandma made a joke about not cutting off my ear, which did not get much of a response.

'You're looking OK on it,' Mum said, stroking my face, 'brave lad. House isn't the same without you, I keep cooking for two, so at least your brother's doing all right off it.'

'Have you remembered to record all of my programmes?' I asked.

There was a TV on a giant, bendy metal arm that you could pull down and watch while lying down, but I was scared to use the remote as it was the same one as for the bed, and as a result had taken to reading.

'Yes, love, I got your list,' Mum said with a hint of sarcasm.

'The rec room's pretty swish,' Chris added. 'I had a neb around while Mum was having a chat with Jackie. We can go down later on if you're feeling up to it. Reckon I could fleece some of those free hot chocolate sachets if nothing else.'

From outside there was more noise than usual as a bustling of feet and voices came down the corridor.

' . . . there are an abundance of herbal remedies, too. I have a friend who deals in Chinese medicine . . . ' I heard a woman's voice saying as she slowly came into view.

'Bloody hell, it's Worzel Gummidge,' Mum said, and Grandma tried not to laugh.

The new arrival did look a bit odd. She had greying hair that seemed to do as it pleased, and flat, sensible shoes that looked like they had survived at least one major war. Her clothes were all rags and materials that flapped and folded around one another in a hundred different colours. On her thin wrist there were what looked like a dozen bracelets, each carrying a different type of stone. 'Well,' she said, as Jackie led them on to the ward, 'I'm glad to see those big windows . . . such beautiful natural light. How fortifying.'

'Maybe so. The sills are a nightmare to clean, though,' Jackie said, leading her towards the bed next to mine.

Two girls followed in their wake. One was younger, and dressed like the woman. The other was around my age, wearing a plain T-shirt and nondescript jeans, with her hair pulled back into a tight ponytail. She looked like she was dressed for a fight.

'You'll be . . . ' Jackie started to say, but was cut short by the eldest girl.

' . . . in the bed with my name on it. I'm there,' she said, hopping up on to the mattress.

'I'll let you get settled in then,' Jackie said, leaving us all in peace.

'Well, isn't this charming?' the mother said to the ponytailed girl, who seemed wholly uninterested. Then the woman turned to us. 'Pleasure to meet you. I'm Colette . . . Colette Spratt.'

'Julie,' Mum said. She went to shake Colette's hand but she ducked the handshake and pulled Mum into a tight hug. I thought Chris was going to pass out from trying not to laugh.

'Isn't this just charming . . . they've gone all out,' Colette enthused.

The eldest girl dragged her dirty rucksack on to the bed and kicked off her Converse before folding her legs beneath her. She turned to us and stared right at me, like she was taking aim.

'I'm Amber,' she said. 'What's your name?'

'Francis.'

'Francis,' she said, as if examining the word with her tongue. 'That's a . . . gentle name.'

'You don't know the half of it, love,' Grandma snorted, and I started wishing Mum had left her at home.

'Shall we close the curtain?' Mum asked no one in particular.

Amber sat cross-legged on her bed and started pulling out all manner of curiosities from her rucksack: postcards and photographs, CDs and old books. Nothing was new, everything cracked or faded and looking like it came with a history.

'You can,' she said, answering Mum for us, 'but it'll be a waste of everyone's time. We'll still be able to hear everything you say. Point well made, though.'

'She's got your number,' Chris said, and Mum glared daggers at him.

'Quite right. We may as well become acquainted,' Colette said. 'Seeing as we'll be bunking down together.'

Amber upturned her rucksack and the rest of the contents scattered messily on to the covers, followed by a fine mist of black dust, which coated the white sheets.

She picked out a giant Toblerone and unwrapped the foil, pointing the stick at Mum.

'Triangle of Switzerland's finest?'

Mum raised one hand and shook her head.

'Francis?' Amber asked.

I said yes and she brought the bar over to me.

'Look at us breaking bread together . . . I like your snazzy jumper,' she said to Chris.

'I've got one just like it,' I said, then felt stupid.

Amber nodded, looking unconvinced.

'Cheers,' Chris said.

'If you ever wanted to buy me an icebreaker, my size is medium. Just saying.'

'Neck of a giraffe, that one!' Grandma said to Colette, who smiled and began picking her way through Amber's deluge.

'Good to know,' Chris said, and took a square of Toblerone.

'Here, new girl, you got any lip gloss? Mine ran out,' Kelly called from her bed.

Amber looked up, but before she had a chance to answer her little sister chimed in.

'Beauty should come from within,' she said, with a wise nod.

'Says who?'

'I'm Olivia,' the kid said politely. 'Nice to meet you.'

'Your trainers are crap,' Kelly snorted, before returning her attention to Amber.

'I don't wear lip gloss,' she said.

'Everyone wears lip gloss.'

'Maybe in your culture,' Amber muttered. 'Come on, Ol, help me with this.'

The other girl did as she was told and began rifling through Amber's assortment of belongings, pinning photographs to the wall above her bed using a dirty clod of BluTack that she had found amidst the chaos.

'Your fly's undone,' Kelly said eventually from across the room, pointing to the white patch of underwear that had begun to poke through the lowered zip of Amber's old jeans.

Amber didn't blush. She barely even moved. She just glanced down at her crotch and then back up at Kelly.

'Yeah, I know, supposed to be. It's mating season,' she said, and then carried on unpacking.

★ ★ ★

In the chill-out room Chris potted a black ball and pretended he had meant to all along.

'I do try making friends,' I told him. Mum must have had a word with him about my lack of socialising on the unit. I sometimes thought she forgot why I was in there. It was the same as when I used to go to youth club. She would always frisk me on my way out to check I hadn't packed a secret book in my coat pocket, even though I was quite happy to buy a ten-pence mix up and sit reading while everyone else played touch football and tried to unhook the girls' bras.

' . . . and I know you're only asking because Mum made you, and that if you were me there's no way you'd talk to people like that either.'

Chris put down the snooker cue and came to sit beside me. Outside some of the nurses were fussing and clanking over the dinner trolley, which meant visiting time was technically coming to an end even though on our ward they were mostly OK with people staying as long as they liked. 'I know. I'm just trying to make it easy on her. She worries. She's talking about redoing the kitchen, so it's new when you come back.'

'That would not help.'

I would need familiarity and stability upon my return, not to enter my front door and be faced with a strange and unknown vista. The sudden change could send me spiralling into a relapse.

'I'll have a word,' Chris said.

'Amber seems OK,' I said eventually, only to try and make him feel better. But he gave me a funny look and shook his head.

'What?'

'She'll spit out your bones,' he said, and laughed.

This was typical of Chris. He could be puerile at times. It was almost impossible for us to watch a sophisticated sex scene in a film together without him guffawing. I remained composed, so long as it was entirely necessary to the plot.

'I don't know what you mean,' I said, and winced, hoping that he would think I was in pain and change the subject. It didn't work. He just carried on.

'*Frankie . . . do we need to have The Talk?*' he asked. I rose above it and did not respond. 'Should I tell Fiona that there's competition? She'll be heartbroken.'

'Don't tell her!' I said, and then regretted it straight away when Chris fell about laughing. He could obviously tell that I wasn't enjoying the conversation as he pulled himself together and then pulled me to his chest in an awkward sort of hug. People kept doing this to me. I did not mind hugs where appropriate — Christmas and birthdays, and following major family bereavements — but since everything kicked off all anyone seemed to do was clutch me to their bosom. It could be quite intrusive at times. On more than one occasion I had considered wearing some of Chris's old spiked jewellery from his short-lived Goth phase as a deterrent.

'You'll be fine,' he said.

I said I knew that to his chest, and could hear his heart beating beneath his T-shirt.

'Do you want me to bring anything in?' he asked. 'CDs? Books? Condoms?'

'CHRIS!' I said, sitting up.

'Come on,' he said, trying not to laugh. 'I'm only doing it for the LOLZ. I'm your king, remember . . . *I brings the ruckus.*'

He stood up and took me by the hands, hoisting me off the sofa.

Back at the beds Amber had headphones on and Olivia sat on the floor reading a book.

'Of course,' Colette was saying, semi-squatting by the side of the bed, 'by the time Olivia came along I had come to know myself and my body so much better, I wanted to be present for each moment of her delivery, and so we opted for a water birth.'

Grandma cleared her throat and looked to the floor; Mum's jaw was hanging open.

'What's all this then?' Chris asked as I settled back into bed.

'Oh,' Colette said, 'just getting to know one another. A brief family history. We're discussing your origins . . . the joy of new life.'

'Oh,' I said.

'And what about you, Mum?' Chris asked. Grandma gave him a gentle kick, which Chris ignored. Mum looked like she was going to launch him. 'Did the joy of new life carry you through the pain?'

Mum breathed out loudly and glared back at him.

'I wouldn't know. You were adopted,' she said with a smile that wasn't really a smile. Grandma laughed nervously and shook her head.

'He wasn't adopted,' she said to Colette, and laughed again. 'You weren't adopted, flower,' she said to Chris, as though he needed reassurance.

'Anyway, I wasn't feeling anything, not from the waist down at least,' Mum said, standing up. 'Full epidural . . . absolute bliss. 'Course, it was the twenty-odd years afterwards I really needed anaesthesia for.'

'Julie!' Grandma said, laughing even more nervously. 'Oh, she's a joker all right, this one,' she said to Colette.

Grandma always cares what people think. Even if she thinks less than little of them, the thought that they may form any ill judgement of her and hers is enough to give her a heart attack. For three years after Dad left for good she told people he'd got a manager's job at head office. Dad has his own business. Everyone knows this.

'Well, we'll be getting off then,' Mum said, kissing my forehead half a dozen times. 'Bye, darling, you take care. And if you need anything . . . ' she said, cupping her hands firmly around my face ' . . . then you just call me, understand?'

I nodded and said my goodbyes.

'Look forward to seeing you again,' Colette said as they left. Mum nodded but did not respond. They weren't even off the ward before I heard her, Chris and Grandma arguing.

Half an hour or so passed and eventually Colette and Olivia made their exit, too. Paul was asleep and Kelly was being wheeled somewhere or other by her aunty who had come on a rare visit, so it was just Amber and me, on our own.

She still had her headphones on so I couldn't start talking to her even though I wanted to, if only so that I could play it cool and prove Chris wrong about everything he had implied.

I started to rearrange my books so the spines were pointing her way, hoping to impress her with the range and depth of my reading matter. I pressed the button on the bed — which Jackie had taught me how to use properly — and felt myself bob up and down like I was riding a wave.

I was just taking out my notepad and pen to make some notes when Amber let out a long and lingering sigh.

'God, I'm booooooored,' she said, half turning her head to look at me. 'No offence, Francis, but your *craic*'s shocking.'

'Sorry. I thought you were listening to music. I'm normally much more interesting.'

Amber shook her head and held up the plug of her head-phones, unattached to her iPod.

'I just put them on to get rid of people. Sort of like your mum's trick with the curtain, only slightly more subtle.'

'Sorry. About Mum, I mean. She's OK really, you just have to get to know her.'

'She's a card.'

I shrugged.

'Thanks for the Toblerone. You can have some of the supplies my Grandma left,' I offered.

'I fully intend to,' Amber said. 'I like your brother, by the way.'

'He's gay,' I said. Then, for no reason at all, added, 'He fancies boys.'

I could tell Amber was trying not to laugh. She did an all right job of it, too. Better than the job I was doing of trying not to blush.

'Oh . . . ' she said, sitting up in bed and turning to face me. '*How . . . exotic.*'

She picked up a grape from the side of my bed and threw it up into the air, swooping her mouth into position so that the grape landed with a popping sound straight at the back of her throat.

'Bull's eye,' she said, proudly chewing. 'So,' she said finally, standing up and tightening the scrunchie around her short ponytail, 'what do we do for fun around here?'

6

Christian was brought in once a week to do a group therapy session, when we were all feeling up to it. He had a naturally soft voice and wore vegan shoes. Amber said his qualifications were probably off the internet. He called himself a healer of sorts. Amber called him something much worse when she caught sight of him for the first time

'Do you feel anger towards your situation?' asked Christian.

He spoke quietly and somehow managed to make eye contact with us all at once. He always started gently enough. During the first session Amber came to he made each of us draw a picture using only six lines to describe how we felt. My talents never did lie in the visual arts so my picture wasn't as accurate as I'd have liked. Then he asked us all to pick a colour that best described our personality. Kelly said pink because it was her favourite. Paul said black and white for football-related reasons. Amber said rainbow because she was 'all about the love' in a voice that suggested she was anything but. I said white, because it was the colour of the gown I was wearing, and I had been sulking since I did so miserably with my mood picture that I couldn't be bothered to participate. Then, after a bumbling lecture on love and positivity, Christian managed slowly to channel the conversation towards our situation, like a bad TV presenter linking two unrelated segments of a show.

'I suppose I do feel angry,' Kelly said. Christian nodded encouragingly. Christian did everything encouragingly. Everything was worthy of reward in his eyes. You'd think this would create a more cheering environment. Really it was just annoying. If even stupid things get praise there's no point in trying to be clever or right. So I just sat quietly and observed. 'Hardly seems fair, does it?' Kelly went on. 'Loads of old people are healthy. And loads of bad people too.'

'I hear you,' said Christian. 'And one point I cannot stress strongly enough is that, no matter how unpleasant, emotions like these should be faced head on — meet them at their level. It can sometimes be too easy to find a culprit and direct all our negativity towards that one object or person, but that isn't dealing with what really matters. There should be no attempt to attribute blame for . . . '

'Oh, you can *always* blame something,' Amber said, interrupting him. Anyone else would have shot her down and told her to let them finish. But Christian wasn't that sort of man. He just smiled and nodded as she gained momentum.

The attention of the whole group turned towards her. Kelly narrowed her eyes but Amber just carried on speaking.

'Yeah, you can blame anyone or anything you like: the government, state education, trans-fats . . . '

'Amber, you're deflecting attention from — '

'Naaaaaaaht!'

'Amber, I understand that at times our emotions can be confusing, and that in an attempt to cope we can reach for an easier, more familiar approach to certain subjects. With you, that seems to be a sort of . . . aggression.'

'No, I'm not being aggressive, I'm being glib.'

'You're being a total cow, Amber. *I* was speaking,' Kelly broke in.

'Can we have lunch soon?' Paul asked.

'Not long,' Christian said, tapping him on the knee.

'Why do you even want lunch? You only chuck it straight up anyway,' Kelly asked.

'Now *that* was a hostile comment,' Amber commented.

'Oh my God, it was a joke!'

'*Christian*,' Amber pointed out, '*I think Kelly's deflecting.*'

'Shut up, Amber! We're trying to talk seriously here.'

'Let's just remember that this is a friendly environment, there is to be no negativity here.' Christian said, looking nervy.

'I reckon she's more scared than she lets on,' Kelly said, trying to get a reaction out of Amber. 'I reckon she acts this way because deep down she's bricking it like the lot of us.'

Christian nodded and turned to Amber.

'Is Kelly's comment something you'd like to address?'

'A census taker tried to test me once,' Amber said eventually, her voice cold and deadpan. '*Didn't end so well.*'

'Fear is nothing to be ashamed of.' Christian was at least persistent. 'If anything it should be celebrated. It keeps us alive.'

'Not me. I'm immune.'

'Why don't you just try and think about it?' he asked. 'Some things must make you scared. Make you sad.'

'Fear and sadness aren't the same things,' Amber said.

'Indeed . . . '

'Oh, loads of things make me sad,' she went on. 'Grown men eating packed lunches, old people sitting alone on park benches,

'Dancing Queen' by ABBA, the video for 'Coffee and TV' by Blur . . . '

'Why do you always have to be the clever one?' Kelly said.

'Same reason you always have to be the thick one.'

'You don't seem to be taking this very seriously,' Christian observed, but with concern instead of accusation in his voice.

'Why should I? I didn't ask for it. I can take it however I like. And anyway, I'm just *sharing*.'

The rest of the session consisted mostly of Christian trying to fill in the awkward silences. Afterwards on the unit none of us said a word. Kelly and Amber never really talked in the first place, not since Amber had erupted on to the ward like Randle McMurphy and upset its natural balance. In school Kelly would have had the upper hand. No matter how much she spat and snarled, Amber would have been torn limb from limb by Kelly and her crew, like a wildebeest calf faced with a pack of lions. But in the real world she had Kelly over a barrel. Every time she said something stupid, which was always, Amber was there to set her straight. Kelly didn't stand a chance. So she sat and scowled, occasionally swearing at Amber when the pressure got too much.

Paul carried on his strong and silent routine. When she had arrived he had glanced Amber up and down, and noticing that she didn't straighten her hair or gloss her lips or scrub herself orange with fake tan, had dismissed her as someone he didn't need to know. She might as well have been invisible. And to Paul she mostly was.

This meant the battle lines were drawn. Amber had me, and Kelly and Paul had one another. This was the set up. And it suited me down to the ground.

★   ★   ★

'Do you want to watch a film?' Amber asked in the chill-out room. We were alone even though Jackie kept popping in to make sure we were OK. All morning I had felt nauseous and weak. My legs and arms would shake when I tried to haul myself out of bed, but Amber had said that the unit was destroying her buzz so we'd moved to the sofas to be alone.

'If you like. They haven't got any DVDs at the minute, though, you've got to use the menu and select one from there.'

'I'm on it,' she said, sitting down next to me.

'Do you think I pushed Kelly too far?' she asked as she scrolled through dozens and dozens of films on the TV, dismissing them one by one.

I shrugged and asked her if she felt bad about it.

'No. Not bad. I just can't stand the crap that seems to be coming out of everyone's mouth. It's not her fault. She's doing the best she can with grim genetics. Christian needs teaching a lesson, though. Same goes for this telly,' she said, although she was flicking so quickly I'm not sure how she could tell. '*Ugh* . . . Titanic . . . *kill me now!*'

I remained silent. You have to pretend to hate *Titanic* for reasons I'm still unsure of as it is probably the greatest romance of our time. Their love was as doomed as that voyage.

'Yeah,' I said. 'That film's the worst. Maybe we could get Chris to bring in some DVDs for us to watch. He has some good ones. Better than all this.'

'Yeah, do it. And get him to bring in some conversation while he's at it. You're killing me here, Frankie,' she said.

'Sorry.'

'I'm joking, you're not that bad. You OK today?' she asked. 'You keep grimacing.'

'I'm fine.'

'Good. Things are a lot more interesting with you around.'

Sometimes I'd catch myself staring at

Amber and only realise I was doing it when she'd throw something at my head — a grape, once, usually an empty pill cup — and tell me to stop being a creep. She didn't look the way most girls did. She was pretty in her own way, with pale skin and big eyes and a mouth that seemed to stretch from ear to ear. Nor did she move the way most girls did. A few years before, when we'd all gone back to school after summer holiday, it was like every girl had been invaded by a body snatcher. They looked the same, but they moved differently. None of them would play any more; they'd stand at the side of the yard, rolling their eyes at everything that happened around them. In lessons they'd sit upright where they always used to slouch, and press their chests up like they were offering them to the Gods.

Amber didn't seem to be aware that she had a body. She would just slump about in whatever position seemed most comfortable. Also she moved her face. The girls at school never moved their faces. They all seemed to spend their time blowing out through their lips in a stupid pout, like they were posing for a profile picture. The effect was off-putting. You could never tell what they thought, for one thing. There was no mistaking what Amber thought. Usually this was because she'd tell you within seconds of deciding herself. But you could see it on her face too, her easy smile and her easier scowl, and the way she'd narrow her eyes at people whenever they talked, as if she was a camera zooming in — closer and closer — until she could see exactly who they were, and exactly what they meant.

'My dad died, you know?' she said as I was studying her face again in the chill-out room. I snapped out of my daydream too quickly, like when you spring out of bed and realise you've forgotten how to walk. I felt my palms become damp and clammy. I had no idea what to say.

I wished she'd just thrown something at my head instead.

'Don't worry. I'm not going to break down on you or anything. I'm just saying, he died, that's why he's not here. And that's why Mum's . . . *Mum*.'

'Sorry,' I said. 'How?'

'Heart attack,' she said, the whole time staring at the TV screen, scrolling quicker and quicker through channels. 'Went to work one day and didn't come home. Mum came to pick us up from school. She got a lift from one of her friends. She can't drive. Well, she won't. Worries about the pollution. But she came in a car that day, and then was silent all the way home.'

'How old were you?' I asked.

'Olivia's age now. Ten. Ol was only in nursery at the time. It was stupid, though. We knew as soon as Mum picked us up that something was wrong. If she hadn't wanted to tell us until we got home, why not just wait for school to finish?'

'Sorry,' I said again.

'You can stop apologising, Francis. I'm just chatting.'

'I know. But it's what you say, isn't it?'

'Suppose,' she said, then turned to face me. 'So I'm just saying, I know what it's like when people die. I know that it's just one less person at the dinner table, and they don't take the whole world with them; it carries on like it always has, only a bit sadder for a bit. So that's why I'm not scared.'

We were quiet again and Amber went back to scrolling through channels. She'd gone so far she was already at the adult ones that you needed a pin number to watch.

'I know what it's like too,' I said eventually. 'When someone dies.'

'Your dad died too?' she asked without looking at me.

'No,' I said. 'He's just not around.'

'Sorry.'

'You don't have to apologise.'

'Just what people say, isn't it?' she said with

a laugh, and put the TV to mute, turning to face me while I told her.

★ ★ ★

Emma died on a day trip to the seaside. She only ran off for a few seconds. She was there one minute, and the next there was just a huge red truck in her place, like she was a Transformer. Only a rubbish Transformer that made everyone cry and Mum howl.

Dad ran towards her and Mum held on to me so tightly that my nose bashed off her shoulder and started pouring with blood. The doctor put a face cast over it and it grew back in a weird shape, like a boomerang. We were seven when it happened. For years I hated Mum because of this. While the face brace was in situ people who didn't know what had happened referred to me as Mankind (we were going through a wrestling phase) but mostly people just stayed out of our way. Mum cried a lot and spent days in bed. On the plus side Chris became brilliant at cook-ing. Some nights he'd do whole roasts, and he made Yorkshires from scratch. Once Emma had been buried and the brace came off, my nose was still wonky, though. I blamed Mum twofold for this. Firstly, because I had inher-ited her Gallic profile. Secondly, for the break itself. But then just after my fourteenth birthday, when Chris found my plastic surgery stash jar, he told me I looked like Serge Gainsbourg and showed me a photo of Jane Birkin. I didn't mind so much after that.

For some reason I felt like such a fraud telling the story out loud. Telling it to somebody else. The way I made some bits bigger than they were; other bits smaller. It was like I was editing a film I'd already seen a dozen times, and even if my audience were none the wiser I'd always know which bits I'd skipped over or which I'd used one too many adjectives on. The whole time I was speaking it felt like I was describing somebody else. I thought I'd be upset. I'd never said it out loud before. Not in so many words. Never needed to. Never wanted to. In the past I'd always been happy keeping myself to myself. But with Amber everything felt different. Like the important bits only mattered if she knew about them. If she'd registered them and stored them alongside her important bits, so that they became important to her too; became her memories. I wanted her to remember the first time she heard about them; where she was when I told her. It was as if, in order to exist, I needed Amber to know exactly who I was, and to know me better than anybody else. Without that nothing else seemed to matter.

Amber seemed interested, and I didn't want to disappoint her. She always looked at you when you spoke. Straight at you, which made you feel like what you said mattered, even if it didn't; as long as Amber was listening there was reason to say it. It was made all the more intense by the way she hardly ever looked at people when she herself spoke. It was as if she never wanted anybody to be able to tell how much of what she said was true. Or maybe how much of what she said she meant.

'So that's why Emma's not here. And that's why Mum's . . . *Mum*,' I said. Amber laughed at this. So did I. It was a pleasing recovery if I say so myself. I was also keen that Amber didn't think I was only telling her to drum up sympathy, or to get even with her for having a dead dad.

'Move over, *Hollyoaks* is on,' Kelly said, making her way into the chill-out room and destroying our moment.

'No,' Amber said. Kelly looked like she wanted to punch her. 'This is our manor now. We're taking over. The geek shall inherit the earth.'

'Eh?'

'Four legs good, two legs bad. *Piss off!*' Amber yelled.

'What are you going on about?' Kelly said, already resigned to having to catch the omnibus on Sunday.

'*Animal Farm*. The underdogs are rising. We're taking over. You'd know that if you ever read.'

'I do read,' Kelly said defiantly.

'What?'

'Katie Price.'

'Oh,' Amber said, chuffed that Kelly was making this so easy for her. 'Well, she is to reading what Quorn is to meat.'

'You're a freak. Everyone thinks so.'

Amber barked at her three times as Kelly wandered off, chuntering under her breath.

'That is how it's done,' Amber said proudly, turning the TV back on.

'You're crazy. You do know that, don't you?' I said.

Amber seemed to take a moment to register the information. She narrowed her eyes, briefly, and furrowed her brow as I began to worry that I'd overstepped the mark.

'You know,' she said, after what felt like an eternity, 'in the olden days doctors used to masturbate crazy women because they thought madness spawned from your fanny, like some really gobby yeast infection.'

Another silence.

I was not entirely sure how to react to this information. Amber was, though. Without warning she leaned over and kissed me on the mouth.

I'd never been kissed properly before. Not by someone who meant it. I can't say I didn't enjoy it, but I wasn't without my reservations. For one thing I suddenly became aware of how empty my mouth was; like some huge cavern that was nowhere near interesting enough for the exploration going on inside. I felt lacking, like I should have had a small petting zoo or firework display going off on my tongue, just to keep the visitor interested. Also our teeth clacked together, and I could hear it magnified in my head. Teeth never seem to clack in films, it's all smooth running there. Ours did. At one point I thought I might have chipped a crown.

When we were finished the room was too quiet even though there were clearly several subjects which needed to be addressed. Amber sat back, closer to me than she had been before but still at a distance.

'Amber . . . ' I said. As the man in our relationship I had decided that it was my responsibility to bring such serious issues to the fore. 'Just to make things clear . . . and there's no pressure . . . but are you my girl-friend now?'

She looked at me and rolled her eyes.

'Wind your neck in, Francis,' she said, and put her hand in mine.

7

Sometimes whole days would be wasted, written off as we lay in our beds after treatment. The whole world would stop mattering to us. All we had to occupy ourselves with was firstly, trying not to throw up, and then perversely trying with all our might *to* throw up, if only to release some of whatever was inside us, whatever made every second for us feel so ghastly it was sometimes hard to breathe.

On days like this Mum would sit beside me for hours on end. She wouldn't go home. She wouldn't even go to work. She just sat there like a guard, taking the measure of everyone who came past the curtain she'd made sure to draw, making sure she knew the exact intention behind their visit and what they had achieved by disturbing us.

During these days she'd rest her hand on mine and whisper things to me while she tried not to cry. Sometimes Chris would come in and sit with me while Mum curled up on the tiny armchair beside the bed and nodded in and out of sleep. He'd take his coat off and cover her with it to stop her from getting a chill. Other times he'd make sure he brought a Thermos and a travel kit he had fleeced off an aeroplane, so that when she woke up she could have a coffee and brush her teeth. All the while they'd be talking to me, talking and talking about things we used to do, about things we were going to do, about things that were happening at home. I would try to answer them but my voice would give way, then they'd pat me on the hand and tell me to rest. It's hard, though, wanting to answer when you can't, like having an itch on your back you can never quite get to. The funny thing is I only ever wanted to say sorry the whole time they were talking; sorry that I was in hospital, sorry that they were there with me. During those days it was as though trying to say sorry was the only thing I could focus on, other than the pain.

Then out of nowhere it would pass. You'd wake up from a nap and suddenly wonder why you felt so different, why the world seemed to be in Technicolor again. Then you'd remember that it was because the pain had gone, even if it was only for a bit, and every second didn't have to be lived through the murky fog of bleak agony.

★ ★ ★

'You had a night of it, brave lad,' Mum said to me as I woke up one morning, feeling fresh after two gruelling days. She moved over to me and helped me sit up, kissing me on the forehead as she did it.

'You smell sour,' I told her.

'I had to use one of those wet wipes Chris brought in. *Zesty*,' she said, propping my pillows up behind me.

'Oh. Where is he?'

'Time off for good behaviour. He's downstairs getting some food. Do you want anything to eat?' she said as Jackie came in to check some numbers on the machine next to my bed.

'No,' I said, feeling my stomach flip.

'You'll have to eat something sooner or later,' Mum said. 'I know, I know, *shut up, Mum . . .* ' she said when she realised that I was not for turning on the subject.

A bit later on I had managed to freshen myself up. Chris had hauled me along to the bathroom and I had used the facilities and splashed my face. When we got back to the unit someone had changed the bedding as the pillow was strewn with stray clumps of my hair. The replacement was a new bright white version, like nothing had happened.

'I brought in my shaver,' Chris told me. Mum turned away and pretended she was looking out of the window but I knew she was crying. 'If you want to get it over with . . . you know, like pulling off a plaster? We can do it together. You do me first, and then I'll do you.'

'But you don't need it. Yours won't fall out.'

'I know, but it'll be fun,' he said. I knew he didn't mean this. Chris was proud of his hair. He had a fringe that he took care of the way Ancient Japanese gardeners took care of bonsai trees. 'Then it'll be like a game. We can race each other to see whose grows back first,' he said, putting newspaper on the floor around the bed.

'Only if you're sure?'

''Course I'm sure, it'll be a right laugh. Some brothers get tattoos together, but we'll be scalped. Now *that's* love,' he said, sliding sheets of newspaper beneath the bed. 'Do you want to go first or shall I?'

I sat up in the bed and spun around so that my legs hung over the side facing Amber, only I couldn't see her because the curtain had been pulled.

'Wait,' I said as Chris angled me so that the back of my head was resting on his chest.

I yelled for Mum to come and open the curtain so that Amber could bear witness to my transformation. Mum did as she was told,

125

and after some coaxing Amber agreed to come and watch. Mum gave her a hand and helped her up on to my bed.

'It's OK. I was reading in one of Kelly's magazines that the convict look is in this season anyway . . . everyone's going wild for Death Row chic,' she said, eating some of my grapes.

'What you chatting about, Amber?' Kelly yelled through from behind her curtain, but no one paid her any attention.

'I think it'll give me a bit of an edge, to be honest.'

'Grrrrr,' Amber said, not entirely enthusiastically.

'I'm just going to get a coffee,' Mum said shakily. 'Does anyone want anything?' she asked, but had gone before any of us had a chance to answer.

'Ready?' Chris asked, ignoring her departure.

I said yes and he turned on the shaver, which was surprisingly loud. I felt it scratch across my head, and felt myself grow colder as wisps of hair fell to the ground like glitter at the end of a concert.

'Going anywhere nice on holiday this year?' Chris asked. I didn't answer him, but Amber and I both started laughing until he got narky and said I was putting him off.

'You have to hold your head still or it'll slip and cut you. The last thing I need is for you to start haemorrhaging on me. It really wouldn't look good on my CV.'

I apologised and he said it was OK, so long as I didn't move my head again.

'In all seriousness, though, I do think I missed my vocation. I am *blitzing* this,' Chris said as he pulled the razor gently from my forehead to the base of my neck.

'Though we wouldn't want to stereotype, would we?' Amber said.

'*Quite*,' Chris agreed, and gave her a wink.

He leaned me over the side of the bed, supporting me with one hand across my chest. With the other he brushed away the stray bits of shaved hair from my bald head. His hand felt odd on my freshly exposed scalp, like I had been lobotomised and he was fondling my brain.

'There, that'll do you,' he said, sitting me back up in bed. 'You think you're up to doing me?'

I looked at Amber and she widened her eyes.

'You know you want to . . . '

I did. I really did.

★　★　★

I pressed it first to the front of his head and began slowly pulling it back from his fringe. The razor made a different sound as it sliced through the first few strands of hair, and became harder to pull. Chris's shoulders tensed as I dragged the blades back towards the crown of his head.

Then I stopped and remembered everything I had meant to say before.

'I'm sorry,' I said, holding the razor tightly in place. 'I'm sorry, I'm really sorry.' I didn't say what for. Didn't say that I was sorry I was ill. That I was sorry he and Mum had to be there all the time, and had to worry all the time. Didn't say that I was sorry that everything had changed because of me, and that Chris's hair was being ruined just because mine was. I just said sorry, and hoped that he'd be able to work out the rest for himself.

Everyone went quiet except for the razor, which kept buzzing like a bee trapped in a jam-jar.

Amber looked at me worriedly and at Chris, who tensed and then flinched.

'It's OK,' he said, holding up his hand and taking the razor from me.

He stood up, still holding the razor against his head, so that I could lie back down.

'Bloody hell, Francis, it's stuck,' he said,

yanking hard at the blades. 'Jesus, it really is! I'm serious . . . '

Amber put her hand over her mouth to stop herself from laughing. Chris yanked at the razor and swore at the top of his voice as it ripped some hair from his head. A smooth runway of pink flesh led from his forehead to the crown of his head.

He grabbed a mirror, looking panicked, and swore again as he observed the damage.

'I'm sorry,' I said between giggles once Chris began to smirk even though I could tell he was gutted. 'I'm really sorry.'

'What's going on?' Mum said, coming back with a coffee. She had put on more make-up since she'd been gone and looked better for it.

'Sweeney Todd here developed a con-science halfway across my skull, *that's what*,' Chris said, slumping down on my bed as he teased his fingers over the bald patch, and grimaced.

Mum put down her coffee cup and stepped back to look at him. Amber had her head in her hands and her shoulders were jigging up and down like she was being electrocuted. Every so often she'd be still and take in a deep breath before carrying on with her hysterics. At first Mum just held her hand to her mouth. I thought she was going to cry again, which would have killed the mood, but instead she smiled, and then let out one sly giggle.

'Sorry,' she said, and then laughed again. 'Oh, you stupid sod,' she said, and burst out laughing, laughing like she hardly ever did, laughing like no one was watching. She laughed so hard she had tears in her eyes, and her nose began to run. Even though she could hardly breathe for laughing she kissed Chris on the head where his hair used to be, then did the same to my head. When she did I could feel her lipstick smear across my skin like a slug's trail.

'My bonny lads,' she said, sitting down on the bed next to me as she tried to get her breath back, 'what am I going to do with you, eh?'

★ ★ ★

That night everyone was quiet. Kelly had been throwing up all day but eventually had settled while her mum and dad were still there. Her dad had left about half an hour after that and her mum went for a nap in the parent's bed, meaning that while we could, technically, still use the rec room, none of us really wanted to for fear of disturbing her.

Outside the lights had been turned off and

the radio had been silenced, which meant that only one or two nurses were still milling about. I felt the darkness press down on me and found myself growing heavier as I began nodding off.

'Francis,' Amber said, pressing her hand to my arm.

'Hmmmm?'

'Francis, are you awake?' she said, shaking my arm so hard that the answer could only have been yes. 'You're going to have to work this for me,' she said, dropping her voice to a whisper halfway through as Kelly groaned and turned over. Amber handed me Chris's razor.

'Have you been stealing?' I asked.

'I asked him to leave it. Come on.'

I said I wasn't sure, that we were supposed to be in bed and a joint toilet trip might incur all sorts of suspicions and reprisals. If they caught us they might have to inform Social Services. I said I thought we'd better do as we were told and wait until morning to carry out any schemes or shenanigans. The rules, I told her, were there for our benefit.

'Oh, Francis ... ' Amber said, piling pillows under my sheets so that it looked like I was still asleep ' ... we all need our heroes. I just wish you hadn't picked John Lithgow in *Footloose*.'

I did not rise to her sniping because it would only have encouraged further insults. But she was obviously ill informed when it came to eighties teen movies set against the backdrop of interpretive choreography. Had she actually watched *Footloose* all the way through then she would have known that John Lithgow comes good in the end. So the joke was really on her.

★　★　★

In the bathroom the long bulb flickered on then buzzed noisily. It was a dirty shade of white, like a towel that had been washed one too many times, and made our skin look even duller than usual.

'I want you to do me too, so that I'm one step ahead of the game,' said Amber once our eyes had grown used to the light and we no longer had to squint just to look at one another.

'But it might not even drop out. It doesn't all the time. It says so in the leaflet.'

'Not a risk I'm willing to take,' she said as footsteps marched lightly past the gap at the bottom of the door.

'Here.' She handed me the razor and sat down on the floor. 'Scalp me.'

In the end Amber took the lead. She pulled

out a pair of tiny nail scissors that she had slid into the elastic of her knickers and started hacking off lengths of her own hair. She used no method or system, just grabbed whole handfuls, pulling them tight from her scalp, and let the miniature blade slice through them until they fell free and drifted around her like leaves in autumn. The whole time she did it I just sat behind her and watched. I remember feeling impressed by how little she seemed to care. Most people doing what she was doing would have shown nerves before the first cut at least. Amber went at the task like it was the only natural solution. She didn't seem to mind one bit. If anything it looked like she was enjoying herself.

By the time she had finished there was hardly any hair left on her head at all. There were only wispy remains, like her skull was growing mould.

'Now it's your turn,' she said, leaning back against me. 'And if you muck it up like you did with Chris, I'll kick your balls back into your stomach.'

'All right,' I said, and turned the razor on and then off again, quickly, panicked by how loud it was.

'What's the problem?' she asked, turning round to face me.

'Someone's going to hear. We'll get into trouble.'

'No, we won't,' she said with certainty. 'If anyone comes knocking, you just start crying and remind them you've got cancer. No one's going to press the subject after that.'

I nodded and she settled down, leaning her head against my stomach once again. I turned the razor back on and, even though I flinched when the buzzing started again, eventually I became used to it and achieved the task at hand.

Amber's few remaining hairs came off in a fine dust that seemed to hover in the air before it settled on the ground around her. By the time I'd finished her head looked shiny but pock-marked, like a dirty moon.

I turned off the razor and put it down amidst the strands of hair on the floor.

'I win,' she said, dragging her fingers across her dented scalp. 'Now come and help me clear all this away.'

★ ★ ★

'I think we've got the thick of it up,' I said after half an hour spent scrabbling about on all fours, trying to reclaim tufts of hair that had stuck to the floor like glued pennies.

'Yeah, it'll do. If anything they'll just think

we came in for a slash and started shedding,' she said.

When I realised she still had her back to me I tucked a small lock of her hair into my pyjama pocket.

'Have you looked at yourself yet?' she asked.

I shook my head. I was fine with being bald, or at least fine with knowing it had happened. I had already gotten used to the extra draught that wafted around my head every time someone opened a door, or the exaggerated shock that occurred each time a drop of water hit my temple. But the thought of seeing myself made me feel uneasy, so for the entire day I had avoided mirrors like the plague.

'Come on.' She gripped my hand tightly and turned us both to face the long mirror on the back of the bathroom door. Neither of us spoke at first. We just stood, hand in hand, staring at ourselves like we'd been painted by the world's most morbid cartoonist.

Had I been on my own I might have cried. I felt my stomach churn when I first caught sight of my reflection. The natural response to seeing a photograph of yourself is to wonder if that is how you always look when you smile, and then vow to remain composed and dignified in public forevermore. This was like that but so much worse. Even with a hat on people would know I was bald. It was written all over my face. But then I glanced at Amber's reflection and realised that she was still pretty, in her own way, and even if she didn't think so, she didn't seem to mind one bit. For some reason this made me relax. I was keen never to cry in front of anyone, save perhaps Mum and Chris. Crying's not the best character trait anyway. It doesn't help that most men seem to cry with a dignified single tear, whereas I start hyperventilating and then wail even louder when I panic about swallowing my own tongue. So it was a relief when it stopped mattering. When everything stopped mattering other than the fact that Amber was there, with me, in the same position, in the same mirror, with the same problems and blotches and baldness, and that she seemed not to care one bit about how she looked. And, perhaps most importantly, that she didn't seem to care how I looked either.

'Well,' she said eventually, her hand still in mine, 'at least there's no chance of us pulling anyone else.'

'There's that,' I said, because it was all I could bring myself to say.

'Cancer . . . one-way ticket to monogamy. They never put *that* in the leaflets.'

'They should,' I said. 'It's always the

negatives they seem to dwell on. I think it's due a bit of good publicity.'

'Innit?' she said. 'Haterz. You're an odd-looking thing,' she told me. 'But I still would.'

I turned and kissed her once on the cheek. It was the first time I had ever kissed Amber. The first time I had ever done anything that she hadn't initiated. The second I did it I felt terrified, like she was going to grimace or wipe it off or say something to cut through the moment, like she always did. But she didn't. She just smiled, and gripped my hand a little bit tighter.

'Come on,' she said. 'Let's get back before we really do get caught. I'd hate people to think I was leading you astray.'

Too late, I thought as she turned off the light and led me by the hand, through the dark, back to the unit.

8

At school we once read a story about a man who buried a body and thought he could hear the corpse's heart beating beneath the floorboards. The sound drove him mad, as well it might, until he eventually confessed everything and ended up getting done for the murder.

I had experienced something similar since what we later referred to as the Great Hair Cull. I'd kept the lock of Amber's hair and tied it into a bow with a piece of ribbon from some posh chocolates Mum had brought when she came from work one afternoon. The idea was that I would carry the hair with me everywhere, so that we would always be together in one way or another. Also it would work well as proof if anyone didn't believe I actually had a girlfriend. The stumbling block was that I never went anywhere, and even when I did make the long trek to the bathroom or the rec room with Amber, I was in my hospital gown, which didn't have pockets. And so my memento of love was kept safe inside the folded page of a book beside my bed. The thought of anyone finding it — most of all Amber — made my stomach cramp with nerves. Every time someone so much as looked at my bedside table I would tremble and get flustered. Once Chris picked up the very book that contained my romantic memento and I almost collapsed. Fortunately he mistook my panic for a 'turn', and dropped it quickly to come to my rescue.

It seemed our love was to be complex and tortured. To research the subject I had asked Mum to bring in a book about the Romantic Poets, to see if they'd had as rough a time of it as I was having. The answer, it seemed, was yes. They also became confused about the use of apostrophes, which was another trait we shared.

'Is 'Bright Star' about sex?' I asked Mum once I'd scanned a few of Keats's poems to catch the gist.

'You'd better not be getting any ideas,' she said.

'I just want to understand them properly. So . . . is it?'

'Oh, Francis, I wouldn't know,' Mum said. ''*University of Life, mate,*'' she added in a Cockney accent.

I told her that after reading some of the poems I had decided that was where I might go too, so that I could sit by a brook and compose sonnets and stuff. Mum told me I'd

139

do as I was bloody well told and that was the end of it.

'Is that the other woman then?' Fiona asked glumly one day when she and Chris came to visit. The curtain around the bed next to mine had been drawn. Olivia sat by the window reading a comic while behind the curtain Colette rubbed healing oils into Amber's skin and opened her chakras. Every so often I could hear Amber mutter something and her mum shush her, explaining that she had to reach total tranquillity for the method to be truly effective.

Some people (Kelly) thought Amber was a real cow. Others (Mum) thought she was a loudmouth smart arse who needed taking down a notch or two. You had to get to know her properly to see that this wasn't true. Or at least that it *was* true, but that there were other aspects to her as well. Like the way she learned everyone's name as soon as she met them, even if it was only to make the insults she doled out like flyers all the more cutting. Or how she would sometimes give people presents from the posters and keepsakes that she kept stuck to the wall above her bed.

Mostly, though, you could see the real Amber by noticing the way she was with Colette. Every time Amber's mum walked on to the unit Kelly and Paul would look at each other with a not-too-subtle snigger. Amber wasn't embarrassed, though, the way most people would have been. She let her mum be exactly the way she was, no matter how much stick by association she herself got for it, and always sat quietly by when her mum went off on some mad tangent — opening her chakras or aligning her energies — and left her to it, even when, if it had been anyone else, Amber would have cut them down to size in seconds.

She'd also become friends with me straight away, which I sometimes think is my favourite quality in people. I'm not saying this to be smug. I just know I'm not the easiest person to make fast friends with. Chris says I'm an acquired taste. Mum once said my gravestone would read: *Worth the Effort*, back when she used to joke about that sort of thing. Amber didn't mind, though. She took me as I was, and the rest is history.

I started to think of her as being like a Magic Eye picture — a jumbled mess that sometimes hurt and often irritated — but if you gave yourself long enough and really wanted to, you could see brilliant things in her. Things that would make you love her, and never be able to stop.

I looked at Chris who widened his hands as if to say sorry. I did not accept his unspoken apology, and scowled to suggest as much.

'Yeah, I suppose.'

'Well . . .' Fiona said, unwrapping a toffee from the bag Grandma had left. 'I can't promise there won't be a scene.'

She popped the toffee in her mouth and chewed down hard.

'You going to leave some for the patient?' Chris asked, as she swallowed and went to unwrap another.

'Comfort eating. For the heartbreak,' she said. 'Besides, I did bring the Lucozade, which was one pound twenty-nine, so it seems only fair.'

After a while Colette left to catch the bus home. Amber's chakras were as open as they could be that day, and she had to get back for a vigil at the church for an asylum seeker who did the dinners at Olivia's school.

Chris had brought in a pack of cards so we started a game of Shithead on the bedspread. Fiona only had three cards left when Amber pulled back the curtain.

She said hello and Fiona introduced herself, pretending to be stand-offish at first but then smiling and moving aside so that Amber could sit in her place on my bed.

'Thanks for the loan,' she said, handing the razor back to Chris. 'What do you think of my new weave?'

'Love it,' he said, trying to sneak a look at

my cards. I am all for fun, but rules are rules so I pressed them to my chest and gave Chris a kick to remind him that I was committed to my role as umpire.

'Oi!' Kelly yelled across from her side of the ward, at no one in particular. 'Here . . . do you know they're, like, *seeing* each other?'

'Are you talking to me?' Chris said.

'Both of you.'

'Hiya!' Fiona said, and gave a smile that I knew was false. Fiona's good at false smiles. I've seen her make a barman whimper on more than one occasion.

'Yeah,' Kelly said, 'they're getting tap. How sick is that?' Amber went to say something but Fiona didn't give her the chance.

'Why's that then?' she asked.

'Because she's bald. It'd be like seeing a bloke. I think it's proper weird.'

'Do you?' Fiona asked. 'Is that what you think? Is that your *really* . . . *interesting* . . . *thought?*' she said, giving Kelly a look that made her shrivel back into her bed like a spider being prodded with a twig.

'Do you want to play?' Fiona asked Amber, closing my curtain to rid us of further interruptions from Kelly then squashing herself back on to the bed, making the sheets tighten around me like I was being

143

mummified. 'You can finish off my cards. I've done most of the hard work for you.'

'Thanks.'

'And don't mind her,' Fiona said to Amber. 'I've seen her type. Before you've finished your GCSEs she'll be eight months pregnant and shacked up with a Bad Uncle. Her opinion's not worth the paper it's printed on.'

Amber shrugged and took the cards.

'Besides, I shaved my head one summer and ended up spending most of September at the GUM clinic. Believe me when I say it's the neck down that holds most interest.'

'Not the mind?' Amber asked.

'Depends on the girl,' Fiona said, downing half the bottle of Lucozade she'd brought in for me. 'Obviously being the world's thickest graduate, I have to rely on the power of my physical allure . . .'

' . . . 'cos it really is the only bullet she's got left,' Chris interrupted, trying to sneak another look at my cards.

'But from what I've heard, you've got nothing to worry about. Francis reckons you're a genius.'

'Comparatively speaking, perhaps,' Amber said, with a sideways glance at me.

'And you've sure as hell got teeth,' Fiona told her. 'Girls like you have nothing to worry about.'

Amber ended up winning in three swift moves.

'Booya!' she said.

Chris said she got lucky that time and challenged her to a rematch. Amber declined, citing exhaustion, but really I knew it was because she wanted to maintain pole position.

★ ★ ★

When I woke up Fiona and Chris had gone and it was dark outside. Jackie brought me some toast but I just nibbled the corner and left the rest for Marc to wolf down when he came to collect the trays. He wasn't supposed to do this but I knew he did, and had written down some rough dates and times in my Diary of Observations in case I ever needed to blackmail him.

'You were KO,' Amber said, coming to sit beside my bed.

'What time did Chris leave?'

'Couple of hours ago. I liked Fiona,' she said. 'As do you, if the rumours are true?'

'Sorry,' I said, and shrugged.

'I'm sure it was just a phase.'

I nodded and didn't dare tell her the extent of my love, which I feared might still be there, deep down. I became quite conflicted until it was time for *EastEnders*, after which all my problems seemed to disappear.

'Shall we put a film on?' Amber asked. 'Mum brought some of my old school faves in.'

'Is *The Breakfast Club* there?' I asked, keen for a launch pad to relay my theory about the unit to Amber — a theory now reinforced by her undeniable likeness to Ally Sheedy. Amber said not, and picked up a stack of boxed DVDs from the table beside the sofa.

'Here, put this on,' she said, handing me a copy of *The Apartment*, which looked to be older than both of our parents put together.

'Is it any good?'

'You'll like it.'

'It looks old. What's it about?'

'A nervy geek who falls in love with a loudmouth harlot. You won't have any trouble identifying.'

'You think I'm a geek?' I asked.

Amber rolled her eyes and perched her legs across me on the sofa.

'She loves him back in the end,' she said. 'Just put it on.'

I had nothing to worry about. The film was excellent, and one to add to my list of all-time favourites. At the end, when you think all is lost, the woman cuts short her date with the wrong man and runs back to the geek's apartment, where he's alone on New Year's

146

Eve. 'I love you . . . ' he says. 'Did you hear what I said? I absolutely adore you.' The woman just looks at him and hands him a pack of playing cards. 'Shut up and deal,' she says, before *The End* appears on screen and everything goes black.

'Have you ever read the Romantic Poets?' I asked Amber once it had finished.

'No. Have you seen *Some Like It Hot?* We should watch that next.'

'In a minute. There's this one poem, 'Bright Star', which I don't think is about stars. I Googled it on Chris's laptop and it's about a bloke watching someone he loves sleeping . . . '

'If I ever catch you watching me sleep, I'll blind you,' Amber said.

'Fair enough. Anyway, he loves her and watches her sleep and thinks she's like a star . . . not because stars are shiny and stuff, but because they're always there, always looking back down and that sort of thing. It's dead good.'

I'd be the first to admit some of its beauty might just have got lost in translation, but the point I was trying to make was valid nonetheless.

'Sounds a blast,' she said. 'Put the film on. We're missing out on some major trans LOLZ.'

As the film began to play she said, 'Do you know the best things about stars?'

'What?'

'They're all dead, but we can still see them. When we look up it's like we're looking up at a million different memories, a million different versions of something that used to be. That's not romantic, either, it's just science.'

'It is a bit romantic,' I tried to argue.

'No, it's not,' she said. 'It's real, and that's what's important.' Then she kissed me on the cheek.

★   ★   ★

The next morning I sent Chris an urgent text message asking for immediate emergency chats. When they say you'll lose your hair you can just about contemplate the thought of going bald. You picture Yul Brynner or Ross Kemp, and think that with the right military uniform or camouflage gear you too could carry off the look, at a push.

What you don't realise is that they mean you will go bald everywhere.

Everywhere.

I spent most of the morning with the sheets pulled up over my head, looking mournfully beneath the covers and remembering what used to be, like the bleak first morning when the snow starts to melt.

'You got something exciting under there?' Marc asked as he did the rounds. I didn't answer. I just snivelled and pulled the blankets farther above my head as I tried to get a better look.

Chris laughed at first when I called him, then tried to be sympathetic. He made a joke about me being more aerodynamic, and I made him promise me that it would all grow back. To put my mind at ease he Googled it for me while I was still on the phone. He even held the mouthpiece to the keyboard so that I could hear him typing.

'Yes, Frankie, the Internet says you've got nothing to worry about.'

'What exactly does it say?'

'That within the month it'll look like you're growing an Afro down there.'

I think he might have been embellishing this point.

'Do you promise? Because I'd rather know if I'm going to have to get used to this.'

'Frankie, relax. It's going to grow back. You've got nothing to worry about. You'll be back to your virile old self in no time.'

This was a joke. And a bad one at that. What Chris singularly failed to realise was that, given the circumstances, I might very well soon be displaying myself proudly, like a lion attempting to mate with the best female in the pack. The thought of having to do so while bald as a baby made me want to sob.

'Well, if it doesn't, I'll blame you,' I said.

'I take full responsibility for all your bodily hair, Francis,' my brother said. 'But I am starting to get looks, so I've got to go. I'll be in tomorrow to see you. Just relax, and say hi to Amber for me.'

Mum spent most of her visit moaning about Grandma.

'It's like she deliberately tries to annoy me, Francis. Thank God you've got me, eh?'

I didn't say anything. Sometimes I didn't know if Mum was joking or not. This was one of those times.

'You've got a delivery,' Jackie said, popping her head round the curtain.

'Who from?' Mum said, and blanched. She hadn't said anything about it to me but the whole time I'd been in the unit I'd known she was nervous about Dad making an uninvited appearance. The last time he'd visited she'd ended up throwing my birthday cake at him before I'd even had a chance to blow out the candles. He'd brought me a card with the wrong age on it, and that had sent her into a frenzied rage. Dad left covered in frosting, and Mum ended up sticking a tea light on top of a muffin as a replacement cake.

'The brother left it,' Jackie said, and Mum relaxed.

'Said he'd be in to see you tomorrow, Francis, but until then this was In Case Of Emergencies.'

The box had been wrapped but bore no tag.

'Open it then,' Mum said.

I did so quickly, holding my hands close to my chest so that she couldn't see the contents.

I was pleased I had done.

It was a long pack from the joke shop behind the bus station in town. Inside was a perfect triangle of crinkly hair. 'Instant Pubes' it said on the box. 'Suitable For Age 12 Up'.

'Let's have a look,' Mum said, going to take the packet from me.

'NO!' I yelled, trying to hold it to my chest. I wrestled her for a while but Mum quickly had the upper hand. I think she would probably beat me in a fight if it ever came to it.

'Oh my God, is that a merkin?' she asked.

'Let's see!' Amber said from her bed, trying to lean over to get a better look.

'It's absolutely disgusting . . . '

'It's just a joke,' I said, trying to pull the sheets back over my head.

'Here,' Mum said, passing the packet to Amber.

'I honestly don't understand you two sometimes,' she continued saying to me. I don't
know whether she meant Chris or Amber
because I couldn't see her. The sheets had
mercifully come loose, and though my feet
and ankles were sticking out I had managed
to shroud my head, cocooning myself from
further embarrassment.

I heard a packet being torn open and
Amber laughing to herself.

'What are you up to?' I heard Mum ask. I
was suddenly becoming claustrophobic in my
place of safety, and tried to make a peephole
with my finger so that I could steal occasional
breaths of fresh air, and also spy on those
around me.

'Just a bit of decorating,' Amber said.

'Oh, nice,' Mum said, trying to pull the
blanket off my head.

I relented, eventually, and slowly peeled it
down so that I could see the whole room again.

'Here, Kelly,' Amber shouted across the
room, 'get your laughing gear around that,
love!'

Amber had pulled the sheets around her as
tightly as they would go so that only her head
was sticking out at the top. In pride of place,
right where it anatomically belonged, the
merkin perched like a dead animal.

'Lezza!' Kelly said.

Mum tutted but I knew she wanted to laugh.

'What do you think of my new do, Marc? Chic, *non?*' Amber asked as he came by to sort out her tablets.

'Ignore them,' Mum said to him. 'They'll tire themselves out eventually.'

'It'll keep you warm if nowt else, flower,' he said, filling Amber's pill cup.

'Practical *and* fancy,' she said, sitting up to take her tablets.

'He's bloody backwards, that lad. Do you want me to take it home and bin it?' Mum suggested.

'NO!' Amber said, cradling it in her hand like a wounded kitten.

'I really don't think . . . ' Mum tried, but Amber interrupted her.

'OH, IT GETS BETTER!' she said, peeling a triangle of plastic from the back of the fanny wig.

'It even sticks!' She turned around in bed and slapped the patch of wiry hair on to the wall behind her headrest, between a photograph of Einstein and a playing card with a phone number written on it.

'We'll love it like our very own,' she said, staring up proudly at her handiwork like it was a priceless work of art.

9

One morning I woke up and Amber was quieter than usual. I tried as always to impress her with my knowledge. I asked her if she knew how many answers the Magic 8 ball beside her bed held. She didn't take the bait but I told her anyway. (It's twenty-one: ten positive, six negative, and five medium.) When this didn't work I decided that maybe it was her surroundings that were getting her down, so I attempted to broaden her horizons by demonstrating my knowledge of the wider world. I told her about the baby sharks that eat one another while they're still in the womb, so that only the strongest is still alive when it comes to the actual birthing. I told her that I always thought of her as the shark that would be born. Like Fiona had said, Amber sure as hell had teeth. But she seemed wholly unmoved by this. Then I told her about Kelly, who'd spent the whole morning trying to do a crossword puzzle in one of the magazines Olivia had left behind. Again there was no response.

'Is it about your face?' I asked when she turned away from me, towards the wall beside her bed. Almost overnight Amber's mouth had become red and blotched, with sores that looked angry and blistered.

'Just leave it, Francis,' she said, without turning to look at me.

'I don't see what the problem is . . . '

'Then there isn't one! Just go back to checking beneath the covers. You might have started sprouting by now.'

'That's not funny.'

'Life's hard.'

'I just didn't think you cared about that sort of thing.'

'It hardly seems fair, that's all,' she said, lying flat on her back and staring up at the ceiling. As she did a single tear welled in the corner of one eye and rolled down her cheek, though she was quick to rub it away like a spelling mistake.

'I still think you're pretty. *I still would.*'

'What's your problem anyway?' Amber said, turning her head and staring at me so coldly I felt myself shiver. 'I'm sure if you try really hard someone else will be willing to overlook you being such a total creep. Do you really think I'd have given you the time of day if I wasn't bald and rotten to the core?'

I did not quite know what to say to this. I knew I wanted to cry. No one had ever before said anything so awful to me . . . Actually that wasn't true. People had said plenty of bad things to me in the past. I went through a ballet phase in middle school which most of my classmates were keen to remind me of at every given opportunity. But in the past name-calling had always seemed like a waste of energy; the sting would have faded away by the time I got home, and then I'd spend the rest of the night wondering why I'd gotten so bothered by it in the first place. With Amber, though, it felt like I'd been winded and would never be able to stand upright again. I felt like I wanted to die.

'I hate you sometimes,' I said. Amber just shrugged as another tear rolled down her face.

★ ★ ★

Unfortunately that day visitors arrived en masse, and even though I made a point of looking dead dour and depressed no one seemed to pick up on just what a difficult morning I'd had. I suppose it was my fault for being naturally so resilient.

Grandma sat in the corner and ordered a cup of tea like she was in a café. Her behaviour was exactly the reason the NHS was buckling beneath its workload. While she was in the toilet I asked Chris to make her bring in a Thermos during any future visits, for the sake of the nation.

'Thank you, love, you're doing a smashing job,' Grandma said to Amy when she brought her the tea and biscuits. Grandma spoke to the nurse like she had just found out she was deaf. She needn't have bothered. Amy had a degree in nursing whereas Grandma left school at thirteen. Amy also spoke better English than Grandma, who was never averse to a double negative.

'I was thinking the white handles, don't you agree, love?' Mum said, waving a decorating magazine in front of my nose. On it there was a picture of a smiling couple in a kitchen so clean it hurt to look at it. I felt myself tearing up, mostly at the thought of how Amber and I would never now be able to pose happily for photographs in kitchen magazines, but also at the realisation of how stupid this couple would feel once they'd realised just how cruel and tortuous love really was.

'It looks stupid,' I said. 'I like the old kitchen. I don't want it to change.'

'Oh, good, we're in *this* mood,' Mum said, flicking rapidly towards the back of the magazine.

To our left Colette was trying in vain to get a response from her daughter. She was halfway through a story about a protest march outside the battered women's shelter when Amber's eyes started watering again.

'Goodness me, what's this?' Colette said, going to wipe away the tears. 'Are you feeling OK? Is it the medication?'

Amber stared up at her and seemed to be saying a million things through two tear-stained eyes.

'Well, this is exactly the sort of thing we've talked about. We must not become defined by our physical selves,' her mother said, lightly stroking the painful rash around Amber's mouth. 'All that really matters is health and happiness.'

'They're two big asks,' Amber said quietly.

Colette looked flummoxed for a moment and started to pull some coloured stones out of a bag.

'Here, let's lay some crystals, see if we can't embrace a bit of positivity. Now, to form an energy grid . . . ' she said slowly, reading a small instruction booklet that was attached to the drawstring of the bag. 'Arms out, darling. We should have you back to your old self in no time.'

She took Amber's arms out from under the covers and spread them flat on the sheet. It was odd, seeing her so pliable. She didn't flinch or scowl or pull in the opposite direction like she usually did. She just did as she was told. I didn't care. I was pleased she was upset, and bald, and ugly. I only wished Chris had visited me on his own, so that I could have told him about my change of circumstances and he could have informed Fiona I was once again single.

Just as Colette was placing the first stone on Amber's arm Mum breathed out loudly, which always meant she was about to go off on one.

'For God's sake!' she said, going over to stand beside Amber's bed.

'Julie!' Grandma said, half laughing the way she always does when Mum makes her nervous. 'Sit yourself down.'

Mum took something out of her handbag.

'She doesn't *need* crystals. And she doesn't need her bloody energies aligning either!'

Mum turned her seat around and sat down close to the bed, placing Amber's hands on the decorating magazine that she spread out over the top sheet.

'Here . . . ' Mum carefully loaded a brush with purple nail polish and dragged it over the nail of Amber's thumb. 'It's been my favourite colour since I was your age. A lot harder to shoplift, too, since they started tagging everything over a tenner in Boot's . . . ' She was moving on to Amber's index finger now.

'You never used to shoplift,' Grandma said with another nervous laugh. 'She never used to shoplift,' she said to me, tapping my leg for emphasis.

' . . . And whenever I was feeling grim, I'd paint it on and look down, and think that if all else failed, at least I had the nicest nails in town,' Mum said, almost in a whisper, as she dragged the brush neatly across every one of Amber's nails.

'I really don't agree with the use of cosmetics,' Colette started to say. 'For one thing there's the animal testing.'

'Shut . . . up . . . Colette,' Mum said slowly, concentrating hard on the task in hand.

'And the misogyny of it all! What's on the outside doesn't matter.'

'Hmmmmm,' Mum said, teasing the brush across Amber's little finger. 'There,' she said, standing back up. 'At least now you know you've got the second-best nails on the ward. You'll have the best once I leave.'

Amber looked down at her hands and smiled, before quickly resuming her scowl as if she'd been caught naked and hurriedly had to cover up.

'You know,' she said to Mum, in a quiet, scratchy voice, 'you're not nearly as bad as you act.'

'Is that a compliment?' Mum asked.

'Closest you're going to get.'

Mum smiled and wiped a tear from the side of Amber's face. She screwed the lid tightly back on to the bottle of nail polish and put it down on the cluttered bedside locker.

'You look lovely,' she said. 'And you owe me fourteen ninety-nine.'

'Well, I can't say I'm happy about all this,' Colette was still saying when Mum sat back down. I saw her face change then. It became harder, like a raincloud had crossed it and you just knew a storm was brewing. The last time Mum had looked like that was when Mrs Pearson from next door came over to complain about the noise from the party Mum had held for her fortieth. Mr and Mrs Pearson moved out not long after that.

'Life's not all crystals and chanting,' Mum said, without turning around.

'Mum . . . ' Chris began. But she ignored him.

'Nor is it lipstick and interior magazines.'

Mum did turn around this time, and glared at Colette.

'Perhaps if you weren't so busy sniffing out causes like some philanthropic truffle hog you'd realise that your little girl's becoming a young woman, and needs to be made to feel good about herself every once in a while.'

'And I suppose you think painting yourself some ridiculous colour is the way to enlightenment?'

'No!' Mum snapped. 'But it isn't half fun.'

'Julie pet, just leave it,' Grandma tried, looking desperately to Chris for further help.

'Seriously, Mum, wrap it up!'

'Perhaps if you'd walked a few days in our shoes you'd realise what really matters in life,' Colette said loftily.

This was the wrong thing to say. Mum stood up like a lightning bolt in reverse. Even Chris looked scared.

'Don't you dare!' she said. 'I've had to bury my own daughter before now, so you can shove the wise old widow routine. You're nothing special, you have no insight, so just get your head out your arse and realise that your little girl needs a mother . . . not some prat with a sack of sage leaves and copy of *An Idiot's Guide to Wicca*.'

'This is not Top Trumps,' said Chris, dragging her back down into her seat.

Everyone fell silent then. That was everyone apart from Amber, who had thrown back her head and was laughing at the top of her voice.

'Well,' Colette said eventually, bending down to kiss her forehead as she settled, 'if nothing else, it's good to see you smile again, darling.' Amber winked at her mum as she started collecting her things together.

'I'll be making a move,' said Colette, placing her bag of crystals inside the hessian sack she'd brought with her. 'There's a bus at twenty-past. I'll see you tomorrow, my lovely girl.'

'*Make it right . . . now*,' Chris hissed at Mum just as Colette was about to leave.

Mum looked sick as anything, but then glanced at me and rolled her eyes.

'For God's sake,' she muttered, standing up. 'You don't have to get the bus.'

Colette stopped in the doorway and turned around. She had started crying.

'Pardon?'

'You shouldn't have to get the bus,' Mum told her. 'We drive here and back every day. We can pick you up. We'll arrange it so we can come together. If you want a lift just wait. One more won't hurt.'

For some reason this really did it and Colette burst into floods of tears. She cried the way I did, all breathless and wheezy, with tears and snot rolling down her face. Mum sighed and then swore as Colette came rushing towards her, arms wide open.

'Oh, Julie . . . ' she said. Mum tried to duck the hug but Colette caught her firmly in her grasp.

'Bloody hell, Colette, you really don't have to . . .'

' . . . it's so important to have friends at a time like this!'

'It's just a lift,' Mum said, trying to wriggle her way out of the hug. Colette must have been deceptively strong, though, as she was having none of it. 'There's really no need to be daft about it.'

'Oh, we'll break the ice yet,' Colette said, eventually letting go of her. 'You're a good woman, Julie Wootton,' she said, still gripping Mum's hand tightly. 'A real inspiration.'

Even though I hated Amber and Chris couldn't stop laughing and Grandma looked mortified, I thought the scene was quite touching. Our families were breaking bread together at long last. For a while our differences seemed to cast the shadow of doom across Amber's and my love . . . back when it still existed. Ours was a family of integrity and tradition, whereas Amber's prided itself on living free. In many ways she was Diana to my Charles. Later, once I'd forgiven her and put this theory to Chris, he made a joke about avoiding tunnels at night and ladies with equine charm. It seemed he had not fully grasped the magnitude of the point I was trying to make.

Later that day, once everyone had gone home, I decided once and for all that I definitely wasn't speaking to Amber and probably never would be again. To begin phase one of my plan to demonstrate as much, I walked straight past her without so much as a glance and stood beside Kelly's bed.

'Hi,' I said.

Kelly did not respond.

'Do you want to play my Nintendo DS? I've got a double lead so we can both play at once . . . I've got loads of good games.'

'Have you been sniffing glue?' Kelly asked, staring at me blankly like I'd just mucked up a card trick.

'No. You can have some of my Lucozade if you like too. It'll be fun. We can bond and stuff.'

'Go away, Francis,' she said, and carried on reading her magazine.

I didn't dare look over at Amber, who I knew was probably watching our interaction like a hawk, and probably loving every second of it too. I had to admit that Operation Make Amber Jealous wasn't going too well. I glanced over at Paul's bed in the vain hope of scoring some points in extra time, but even I

165

wasn't that desperate, so returned to my bed, forlorn, and pretended to go to sleep.

'Are you still cross with me?' Amber asked. I remained silent and wounded, refusing even to glance in her direction. 'I'm quite upset too now, Francis, especially with you and Kelly getting on so well.'

I still didn't look at her but I knew she'd be smiling. I had never hated Amber more than I did at that moment.

'In fact, I think I might have my yoghurt now, to try and cheer myself up.'

I glanced over at Amber as she peeled open the tub left over from lunchtime.

'Do you want to lick my lid?' she asked.

I didn't say anything so she held out the tub and brandished it at me. She'd spent the whole evening biting at her nails and picking away at her cuticles, so already the varnish was chipped and cracked like army camouflage.

'*Finger my pot?*' she said, and laughed. I turned over so that I was facing away from her.

No one said anything for a while, and eventually I felt a weight press down on my bed as Amber sat on it and tucked her legs beneath her. She stayed quiet as I lay there, trying not to turn over and look at her, then suddenly the whole bed started shaking.

166

'Will Francis and Amber's glorious love story resume?' she asked, shaking the Magic 8 ball over my head.

'It is decidedly so,' she said.

The word love certainly made me cock my ears. It even made me reconsider the possibility that perhaps Amber wasn't the single worst person who had ever lived. But I played it cool and stayed, curled like a foetus, not looking at her, to see where she was heading with her routine.

'Well, that must be right,' she said. 'I knew there was something in all this fate business. As far as I'm concerned that was six ninety-nine well spent.'

I smiled but didn't turn around so she couldn't see and it didn't count.

'Tough crowd,' Amber said as the bed started shaking again; harder this time, like we were being mutually possessed.

'Will Amber ever say sorry for being a total cow and upsetting her fave?'

I turned my head but not my body so that I could see her, jigging up and down on my bed as she furiously wielded the ball from side to side.

'Come on, Francis . . . almost there . . . rub it for luck.'

I lifted my hand from the bed and brushed it against the ball, still unimpressed.

'The stars say no,' she announced, as the bed stopped shaking. 'Suppose you can't win them all.'

I decided to make things slightly easier for her.

'I'm your fave then?'

'Don't be such a woman, Francis,' Amber said, rubbing her hand up my back towards the nape of my neck.

Then, with a smile, she started shaking the ball again with all her might.

'Will we ever get out of this ward alive?' she asked, waving the ball closer and closer to my face.

'Don't!' I said, pressing it away so that she couldn't see the answer. Unable to gauge the reaction of her audience, she smiled and carried on.

'Will Amber and Francis be immortalised in death like Romeo and Juliet or similar . . . ' she asked, shaking the ball again.

'DON'T!' I said, getting up and pulling it from her hands.

In fairness she did look like she was feeling sorry at this point, though of course she didn't say so. Amber never apologised. She played games so that you knew she was, and then picked and teased at the word, venturing close though never fully engaging with it, like a fat person with a too-hot sausage roll.

'Will Amber ever learn to give it a rest and let Francis have an easy life?' she asked one last time, shaking the ball furiously. 'Concentrate and ask again,' she said, holding the ball up to her face.

Amber slowly moved across the bed so that she was lying flat next to me. I could feel the skin of her arm against mine, and her breath tickling the back of my neck. Because of this I became unable to turn over for all sorts of reasons.

'If I promise to concentrate really hard in the future, will you be my friend again, Frankie?' she asked.

At this point, I decided to relent. Plus my earlier interaction with our companions in the unit had made me realise I really had burned all other bridges.

'All right,' I said. 'But I never said I wanted an easy life.'

'Go on . . . ' she said, curling closer to me.

'Because I like having you around. I like having you around more than I've ever liked having anyone around . . . ever. Just don't be a dick!'

'Deal!' she said, and kissed me on the lips.

'Deal!' I said, and kissed her back.

'Hurray . . . ' Amber whispered, pushing my mouth into an awkward smile. 'Kodak moment for Mickey and Mallory,' she said, as the Magic 8 ball fell out of her grasp, and rolled into the last few inches of space left between us.

★ ★ ★

On my last night Kelly had been groaning for hours on end. She had lost her hair too but hadn't learned anything from the experience. She would still try to glance at the footwear or accessories of the doctors and nurses frequenting her bedside, and form all character judgements based on her findings.

'Why don't you ever try with Dr McCallum?' Jackie asked one day after Kelly had remained mute throughout one of his routine check-ups.

''Cos he's only got a Nokia 3210 . . . *the bell-end*,' she said, before snorting a cheap laugh then returning to her magazine.

In the middle of the night I heard her throwing up in the toilet. She had left the door open. For attention, I thought, and put a relaxing song on my iPod to try and lure me into sleep.

Halfway through the second verse of 'Orinco Flow' I caught a glimpse of a shadow walking past my bed. At first I thought I might have been tripping from the zoned out playlist Chris had made for me. When I

170

realised this wasn't likely I just assumed I was hallucinating. Mum told me that when I had meningitis I'd carried out an entire conversation with a Rosie and Jim poster on my bedroom wall, so I knew I was prone to such flights of fancy.

Then I saw the way the shadow shuffled and slumped down the length of the ward, and realised even a mind as unconventional as mine couldn't have invented a character so formless. It was Amber, I realised, making her way sleepily towards the toilet.

Before I had time to turn off my iPod I saw her go into the bathroom. She was there a while, as Kelly retched and gagged and sniffed back tears. I heard Amber speak but couldn't tell what she was saying. She talked longer than she ever had to Kelly before. Usually they spoke one line at a time to one another. And usually even that was an effort. But Amber seemed to be talking at length tonight, just quietly whispering things that I couldn't make out. They were in there so long that I thought perhaps she was happy to have finally made a female friend to discuss our blossoming love with. Kelly seemed unresponsive at first so I assumed Amber was waxing lyrical about our time together. I sat up to try and have a better listen then slid back down into pretend sleep when I heard Kelly mutter something in response, and then the sound of the bathroom light being turned off.

When they came back they were together. I'd muted my iPod so that I could hear all that transpired, but kept my eyes closed to maintain the illusion.

I heard Kelly being tucked back into bed, and someone filling a cup for her from a jug of water.

'Thanks,' Kelly said, tearfully. Then, I assume to maintain the status quo, she added, 'I still hate you.'

'Good,' I heard Amber say as she made her way back across the ward. 'Don't be getting any funny ideas either. This doesn't make us friends. You haven't even got a library card.'

'You haven't even got a BlackBerry. *Tosser!*' Kelly said, as Amber climbed back into bed.

★　★　★

The day I left the unit Chris helped me make a Get Well Soon card for Amber. We printed it on to a sheet of card backed by a photograph of the constellations. On the reverse we'd printed the poem 'Bright Star' in special, swirling writing.

'Is this a thing now?' Amber asked, turning the card over and looking at the poem, bemused. All I could assume was that in her drugged-up state the subtlety of the gesture had been lost on her.

'Yes. I told you about it. Remember? It can be *our* poem. It is a thing. Honestly.'

'Fair enough. I like it.'

'We invented the font ourselves,' I told her proudly while Mum hovered at the door of the unit, chatting to Jackie. In truth, now that I had found Amber I wanted to stay there, but didn't dare admit as much. Nor did I tell her that when I said 'we' had invented the font, I'd really meant Chris, who had brought his laptop and printer to the unit that day so that we could sneak off and make this token of my love in secret. I'd simply stood over him and told him it was rubbish and that he'd have to do it again . . . until I was as pleased with the last-minute effort as I could be. 'We named it after you. It's called Amber Sans. Chris wanted to call it Gobshite Gothic, but I said not.'

'I love it,' she said eventually, pulling off a clod of BluTack and pinning my card to the centre of the arrangement above her bed. 'I didn't get you anything, though. My presence is a present, I suppose.'

This was true. But a real present wouldn't have gone amiss. I'd mentioned on more than one occasion how partial I was to iTunes vouchers.

'Here, have this,' she said, peeling off her plastic wristband and handing it to me.

'You're supposed to keep that on,' I said, hurriedly shoving it inside my pocket.

'What? For when they identify the body?'

'Don't say that,' I said, and Amber made a joke 'sorry' face and then squeezed my cheeks into an uncertain smile.

She seemed to find it amusing when I asked her what she was going to do without me. In fact she laughed solidly for almost a whole minute. I counted. I don't know why. Already I knew that my days would be wasted without her. She was like my strongest limb; without her I would be lost.

'I think that, hard as it is, I will just about cope . . . with the support of friends and professionals.' She said this with an expression so serious it must have been a joke.

'But who'll you talk to?'

'Oh, I don't need friends. And if I do there're always options. Here, Kelly . . . ' she yelled across the ward. 'What are the chances of you and me becoming bezzies? There's an unexpected vacancy.'

Kelly flipped Amber her middle finger without looking up from her magazine.

'Besides, it'll be fine. It takes up most of my time being totally unreal anyway. I've become pretty lax what with all the *Together*

Time. I'll probably just concentrate on getting back to my former level of ace-ness.'

'Hair!' I said.

'Hah,' she said, squeezing my hand.

I kissed her goodbye quickly when nobody was looking and left her alone before she had a chance to get too tearful at the thought of life without me. The whole morning she had done an admirable job of putting on a brave face, right down to the nap she had pretended to have when Jackie brought in the cake and juice for my somewhat paltry leaving party.

★ ★ ★

'You ready, big lad?' Mum asked as I made my way over to where they all hovered at the doorway.

'Suppose so.'

'You watch how you go, flower. Though no doubt I'll be seeing you again,' Jackie said, giving me a hug.

'Tomorrow,' I told her.

'We'll see,' Mum said. She was yet another obstacle I would have to defeat in the name of true love. In fact, she was the main obstacle. That and nausea.

'Well, you've done very well, my love. You're a good lad, Francis Wootton,' Jackie said, kissing my cheek.

When we got home Mum had put up balloons and Welcome Home cards, most of which were from her friends and seemed more for her benefit than mine.

'Did any have money in?' I asked.

'It's not Christmas, Francis, it's a goodwill gesture. It's nice that people care,' she said with an unusually nervous laugh, unpacking the various packets of pills. I glanced back over the cards. There were eight in total. Some of the handwriting looked remarkably similar, and they were signed by people whose names I didn't recognise. I think Mum might have got some of the girls in the office to write out duplicates, so that I would feel as though my health concerned more people than it actually did.

'Do you want to see anyone today?' she asked.

By 'anyone' Mum could only have meant Chris and Grandma. And she must have known my answer would be yes.

'Well, I'll cook something nice,' she said. 'I bought all your favourites. I didn't know if you'd be up to food though so it's all in the fridge just in case.'

After that we didn't say anything for a long time. There was something different about being home. It was as if it wasn't so secure any more, not so solid as it had once seemed.

Like it had done when Dad had left for good. Suddenly it felt like a mirage; like if I concentrated too hard it might suddenly disappear and I'd find myself back on the unit. I don't know why this was. I was pleased to be back. But for the first few moments it felt as if I was just visiting, as though I would now have to ask if I could help myself to a drink, or if anyone would mind whether or not I drank the last of the juice in the fridge. It was as if I'd outgrown my old life and returning felt like a strange exercise in nostalgia, like the times I'd look up songs on the internet that I remembered from youth club.

It was not a sensation I enjoyed.

I think Mum might have been feeling something similar because she was more cautious around me at first too, as if we'd just had a really huge argument that had been all her fault. Even in the car on the way back she hadn't rolled her eyes or snapped at me for being stupid when I'd talked without pausing for breath about my plans with Amber. And once we were back inside she stood at least two paces from me, whereas in the past she'd never concerned herself with the notion of personal space, no matter how often I requested that she would.

After what seemed like an impolite stretch of silence Mum looked like she was going to get upset again, which was the last thing I needed. But then she smiled, and came stomping back over to me like she always did.

'I am so happy you're home,' she said, making each word very clear like they were being chiselled into a stone tablet. 'I love you so much, Francis. Really I do. And I'm so, so proud of you,' she said, hugging me harder and harder until it began to hurt a bit.

★ ★ ★

For weeks I didn't leave the house much. Time itself became distorted and unreliable. Without the structure of school, or hospital, and on those days when I couldn't even be bothered watching TV, I lost all concept of minutes, hours and days. It would have made little difference to me anyway. I did the same thing whether it was six in the morning or eleven at night: I felt lousy.

My visits to see Amber were restricted to a minimum, if they were permitted at all. And on the odd day that I convinced Mum I was well enough to leave the house, Amber would be mostly unresponsive. She would just lie there, weakly attempting to spit out one-liners while the medication tore through her body like liquid sandpaper, leaving her raw and frail.

I spent most of my time in bed. I'd pick up a pen but had nothing to write. I'd pick up a book but the words just became dead weights; an extra burden on a mind that already felt over-charged and spent. And so I lay and wallowed as Mum tried to perk me up.

One day Jacob came to visit, which did more harm than good. In the months I'd been away he had been slapping through subjects along with the rest of my class, to the point where I began seriously to worry that he might be on his way to becoming my academic equal.

'What's the capital of Peru?' I asked, halfway through his description of Jenna Bowley's left boob, which he'd only seen thanks to a wardrobe malfunction during double swimming.

'What?'

'The capital of Peru. What is it?'

'I don't know,' he said. 'Anyway, so it was a bit bigger than it looks in her jumper, but whiter than her face is. She looked like an upside down pint of Guinness . . . '

Jacob went on but I stopped listening. I was just pleased that the natural order had been restored.

(It's Lima, by the way.)

Jacob also told me that in my absence he had taken to hanging around with Nick

Tilley. For a while nobody would speak to Nick because we found out his big sister was really his mum and the information blew our minds. He had conducted his campaign well, though, and ended up triumphing when, that September, he'd returned to school with a tattoo and a prescription for antibiotics after having done something heroic with his foreign exchange student.

That said, I don't think his and Jacob's friendship was as solid as Jacob was making out. He talked about what they'd been up to together with a sense of urgency in his voice, like if he didn't keep saying it then it wouldn't be true. Whereas I only mentioned Amber once or twice, which in itself was testament to how strong our bond had become.

★　★　★

The nurse came round once a day. For a while nothing happened. If anything I got worse. All day and all night I could hear the inhuman sounds I was making, like they were coming from a stranger, as Mum held the bucket beneath my dribbling chin and whispered kind things about how well I was doing, that even she didn't sound convinced by. Then after a while things changed. Slowly at first, like the last days of winter. There would be moments where I'd feel OK. Then the moments became hours. Until eventually there were whole days, sometimes two on the trot, where everything seemed better.

The nurse started using words that I recognised from television. At first it was that the medicine was 'taking', which made me feel like a Crazy Golf windmill with each pill being putted at my mouth. Then I was 'responding well'. Which meant that I wasn't throwing up and could mostly go about my daily business without having to take naps to recover from the previous nap, or throw up every time there was a change in temperature or someone within a five-mile radius was cooking food.

Grandma would come and keep me company when Mum had to do urgent work tasks at the kitchen table. She'd sit by my bed and tell me about her day, and when I could take no more of such cruelty I'd ask her to start reading to me from one of my books. She seemed happy enough to do this at first; only halfway through the first chapter she'd go one of two ways. Either she'd nod off in her seat and slump face first on to my bed, so that I'd have to try and nap without kicking her in the eye, or else she'd purse her lips, and suck in each intake of breath while she cleaned up the language and skipped over the good bits of some of my favourite novels. I don't think Grandma was ever open to the idea of experimental fiction. Her house was full of books with jacket artwork featuring pleasured-looking women staring out from under floppy fringes. Almost all of them had lavender-coloured backgrounds. I think she picked them to match her dado rail. One afternoon I gave her a selection of books that I thought might open her mind and improve her, both academically and culturally. The next morning Mum came into my room looking furious as hell. It seemed Grandma had not taken too kindly to *Naked Lunch*.

★   ★   ★

Otherwise I spent most of my time texting Amber to apologise for the iron fist that ruled over my first few weeks at home. I tried pleading with Mum for greater liberty, but she was immovable on the subject. I told her that they had medicine for what was wrong with me, but there was no known cure for a broken heart. This only made her hyperventilate then kiss me between giggles, while thanking me for the first proper laugh she'd had in weeks.

Once I was feeling better Mum agreed that I could visit Amber occasionally, so long as she accompanied me in case I took a turn for the worse.

'But there are doctors and nurses there if anything happens,' I pleaded, I thought reasonably. But Mum was not for turning.

'Those are my conditions, so like it or lump it.'

*   *   *

The first time we visited the nurses crowded around me and made a big fuss. Amber looked dead sick.

'It's like you get off on being the Golden Boy,' she said sourly once Mum had gifted us with a few unsupervised moments and gone to fetch some teas. I couldn't help it, though. Often my natural charm prevailed despite myself. Also it might have had something to do with Mum. She'd paid for all the nurses to have a spa day in town as a thank-you present. When we arrived Amy and Jackie both had long, colourful nails with jewels stuck to them. I voiced my concern with regard to Health and Safety to Amber, but she just swore at me.

'Is Paul still staging his dirty protest?' Amber asked as she washed down her tablets with one deep gulp of water. Paul wasn't on the ward that day. Apparently he'd spent most of the night throwing up and worse.

'He's doing OK,' Marc said. 'And go easy on him. Last thing he needs is your smart mouth when he gets back.'

'I can't help it. It's just the way I spit my lines,' she said as Marc took her empty cup and left us to it.

Amber said that it was boring on the unit without me. I smiled. I had come to realise that relationships were all about reading between the lines. So when she said it was boring without me, it meant that she missed me. When she told me I was being a creep, it meant that she found my behaviour adorable but was frightened to render herself vulnerable by acknowledging the attraction she felt. It was probably my ability to analyse such subtle quirks that made me such an ideal boyfriend.

'You look like you're having a stroke,' she said, punching me in the arm as I beamed out of the window. I had obviously underestimated the effect I had on her. Amber was smitten. I was her drug of choice.

When it was time for me to leave I gave her a £10 phone card that I'd used some of my savings to buy and told her to text me whenever she could. She said she would, and then, out of nowhere, added, 'You are coming back, though, aren't you?'

I told her I would, and saw a strange look on her face then, somewhere between gratitude and relief, neither of which were expressions Amber wore frequently (or well).

'She's not as tough as she acts, that one,' Mum said proudly, like her hypothesis had been proved, as we made our way out of the unit after saying goodbye.

Before we made it into the car park my phone buzzed and I opened the message. It was from Amber.

Not that I care or anything x x

I kept it to myself, even though showing it to Mum would have proved her to be wrong.

10

During my visits to the unit I would watch Amber peak and trough like a human rollercoaster. Sometimes she'd be sprightly and responsive, her cheeks flushed with colour, like she was crawling out of the cocoon of her own disease. Other times she'd be silent, sallow and sickly, and barely able to lift her head without every muscle in her body shuddering in pain.

I'd try to keep her upbeat with my many interesting stories and lesser-known facts about eighties teen films and seventies rock bands. But such was the extent of her suffering that sometimes even this would make little difference to her mood.

The one constant that seemed to keep her going — other than tormenting Kelly and making snoring sounds whenever I had been talking for too long — was the oft-postponed promise of her homecoming. The idea was that she would spend some time back at Colette's house, in her own bed, and receive daily visits from a nurse while she took her treatment in a more familiar environment.

'They just can't get enough of me here,'

she'd say when the plan was shelved yet again. 'They're like the Spice Girls and I'm Geri. Without me they're just a joke.'

'It's not that bad here,' I'd say, frantically seeking out positives. 'At least they've got Sky Plus. And meat. At least it's not all Quorn and herbal tea. You never know, all the protein might shock your system into getting better.'

'Somehow I think it's going to take more than a Fray Bentos to do the trick,' she'd say dourly, teasing the Magic 8 ball without asking it any questions (which must be bad luck, confusing the cosmos as it would).

Sometimes I think she noticed just how sad she could make me, and to try and lessen the damage she'd pick up her mood like a weighted rucksack and start making jokes again.

What she didn't realise was that this was worse again. The whole time I'd known Amber on the ward I had never known her to put on a front for anyone. She was like a human emoticon; she wore her mood like a T-shirt slogan, no matter how it jarred with the rest of the ward. I myself was quite adept at hiding my true feelings, and consequently people often overlooked just how burdened I felt, what with having cancer and being in love all at once. But not Amber. Her mood was written right the way through her.

Except on those days. Those awful days when she'd joke for me but her eyes looked like they belonged to someone else; looked like they knew something the rest of her body wasn't yet willing to acknowledge.

★　★　★

One day I woke just after eleven and made my way downstairs, shakily.

'You all right, darling?' Mum said, helping me on to the couch.

'Yes. Just dizzy.'

Mum went into a flap and dropped my medicine box twice while she was looking for the right tablets. She threw the pills down me and began pressing her hands against my throat and head.

'Have you got a temperature? Can you see me OK? Do you feel right? Shall we get the nurse just to check you over?' she asked without pausing for breath.

'No . . . get off,' I said, pulling her hands away from my face. 'You're just going to have to help me get ready, that's all. I said I'd go in at one o'clock today.'

'Oh, no,' Mum said, shaking her head and covering me with a blanket. I kicked it off but she threw it back over me and pinned the corners down, afterwards kissing me on the head. 'You can hate me all you like, but you're staying here today. No discussions.'

'You got the first bit right,' I mumbled cruelly as she went to make me breakfast. I felt bad as soon as I'd said it but she deserved to be punished for standing in the way of true love.

'She's certainly bringing you out of yourself, I'll give her that,' Mum said as she screwed the cap back on to my medicine bottle.

I spent the entire day on the sofa, Amber's lock of hair hidden in the pocket of my pyjamas, watching *Titanic* and other films about love against the odds.

Fiona tried to perk me up by showing me clips of sickening films on her phone. Even the ones that I found amusing, I refused to respond to. I would turn my head away like I was on hunger strike, making it clear to all and sundry that I was lovesick; there was no cure for my ailment.

'Give it up, Frankie. You and I both know you'll be back there tomorrow. It's no drama. It's just one day,' Chris said.

'It feels like a lifetime,' I replied, sliding further down the couch until I could only just make out the top of Kate Winslet's nipple. 'And anyway, you'd be miserable if Mum was

189

ruining your entire life and any possibility of future happiness.'

'Yes,' Chris said, 'yes, I would. But I hope I'd have the good grace to come out with a bit of banter. My personality would shine through even the deepest caverns of despair.'

'Well then, you *obviously* have never been as miserable as I am. Because even breathing hurts when I'm not with her,' I said, and he laughed. Sometimes I wonder how I ever endured such an upbringing. I was like the solitary flower sprouting from an endless stretch of cold, hard concrete. Perhaps my biggest problem was that I bore the burden of emotion for the whole family. Like all great poets my downfall was that I simply felt too much. 'Oooooooh,' I groaned when Fiona and Chris began a conversation between themselves, paying no further heed to my plight.

'Frankie, pull your finger out and get up,' Fiona said eventually, slapping my legs. 'I've shown you all my best films and relayed both my best stories and, to be honest, I'm starting to take it personally. We all know you love Amber but the whole injured dog routine's getting you nowhere.'

'I don't know what you mean,' I said, sitting up grudgingly. I have never responded well to tough love. I take better to cosseting, and sometimes Grandma was the only one who could step up to that particular challenge.

'Well, for one thing, you're being a berk. For another, absence makes the heart grow fonder, so she'll be doubly pleased to see you when you do make it, and will probably show you a boob or something in gratitude.'

'Keep talking.'

'And every time you make the sound of a yak being branded, no one knows whether it's the hysterics of a lovelorn teenager or the pained cries of a cancer patient . . . and you know it. So cut it out now.'

'Some of them were real cries of pain,' I mumbled.

'Really?'

'Well, not pain. Mild discomfort.'

'Remember what happened to the boy who cried wolf?' Fiona said. 'He was eaten alive. Do you want to be eaten alive?'

'I suppose not.'

'Then stop winding everyone up.'

★ ★ ★

I perked up a bit after that but still insisted on watching maudlin films to mirror my mood, so Chris and Fiona had to endure *Romeo + Juliet* and we were halfway through *King Kong* when Mum came in with sandwiches and refreshments.

191

'Still the Weeping Wives Club, is it?' she said, putting the tray down on the coffee table and collecting the used tissues and sweet wrappers that carpeted the floor beside where I lay curled on the sofa.

'We're having a dark day,' Chris said, and threw a heart-shaped Haribo across the room so that it bounced off my head.

'Leave him alone,' said Mum, biting into a sandwich. 'Are you two staying for tea because I'm getting a takeaway?' she asked.

Fiona answered yes for both of them just as my phone began vibrating on the coffee table.

'Beaten!' Chris said, darting across and grabbing it before I had the chance.

I yelled at him, trying to grab the phone, but he kept jerking his arm and holding it behind his back.

'Are you going to cheer up now?' he asked, switching the phone from hand to hand, passing it behind my back and holding it above my head.

'YES!' I cried, trying frantically to steal it back.

'And concede that I am the single best brother in the history of the world ever?'

'YES!' I said, becoming more frantic as Chris shook the phone in my face then held it behind his back.

'Now, describe my hair using at least six

adjectives,' he said.

'Somehow I always knew it would come to this,' Fiona said, but I was too angry to respond.

I punched him in the arm and tried to tease the phone from his grasp but he wasn't giving in.

'Mum . . . he's inhibiting my recovery!' I whined.

'Give him his phone, for God's sake, Chris. I can't take another verse of 'My Heart Will Go On'.'

Eventually he relented, handing my phone back to me.

'This isn't over,' I muttered as my fingers stumbled over the keys, trying to open the text like it was a Christmas present I knew I was getting but urgently needed proof of.

When I finally managed to access my inbox I could feel the smile spread across my whole face.

'What does it say?' Fiona asked.

I didn't answer. Just held up the phone to Mum, allowing her to read the three most beautiful words in the English language.

I'M BACK, BITCHES!

The next day I was feeling mercifully better and after a morning of intensive negotiations with Mum, and at least three unnecessary phone calls, she finally agreed to let me spend the afternoon at Amber's house.

'I just want to make it crystal clear that I am not happy about this one bit,' Mum said in the car as we pulled on to Amber's estate.

'You mentioned that,' I said dreamily, focusing my attention on each inch of the road, trying to absorb it faster and faster so that we'd arrive as soon as possible.

★   ★   ★

'Are you wrapped up?' Mum asked as we got out of the car.

'Yes. I'm fine. Just be nice.'

'Don't push your luck,' she said as we knocked on the door.

Colette had made a tray of biscuits and the whole house was filled with balloons and streamers for Amber's return.

'We had a little party last night. Nothing too extravagant,' she said when she answered the door and pulled Mum into another stealth hug.

'Hello, Francis,' she said, kissing my cheek. 'Aren't you looking well?'

The house was scorching. Mum had to take off almost everything she was wearing while she stayed for the good-behaviour cup

194

of tea that she had promised me she would. Amber later told me it was because Colette had taken to Bikram yoga in an attempt to strengthen both body and mind. If you looked closely you could sometimes see small scars and scalds on her ankles when her skirt rode up above her socks. She told people they were from the time she had walked across hot coals at a women's empowerment retreat. Really they were because she kept relaxing a little bit too much when she did 'Corpse' and catching her feet on the three-bar fire.

'Are you sure you don't mind having him?' Mum asked as I sheep-dogged her out of the front room towards the door.

'The more the merrier. There's always room at the inn,' Colette said, and patted me on the shoulder.

'I don't like leaving him, you know, not just yet.'

'I'm fine,' I said as Amber stretched her leg across the couch and dug her foot into my stomach, making stupid faces as she pressed harder and watched me wince.

'Just make sure you are. This is my landline, and my mobile number in case the line's busy,' Mum said, handing Colette a sheet of paper. 'And he's got his medicine and knows when to take it, but just make sure he does.'

'Of course. We'll be all hands on deck, eh, troops?'

'It's good to see you well, love,' Mum said to Amber, taking a small, wrapped present from her handbag and leaving it on the mantelpiece. 'Just a little something in case you ever need it.'

'Well, isn't that just adorable?' Colette said, swooning over the present, which looked average at best to me.

'Thanks, Julie. And thanks for letting Francis come, I know it's a big deal,' Amber said as Mum came back into the room to kiss me goodbye once more.

'I'll be back at five,' she said before finally making her way towards the open front door.

'Well,' Colette said, coming back into the front room after waving her off, 'isn't this cosy?'

'Haven't you got some pottering to do, Mum?' Amber said eventually, and Colette took the bait.

'Of course. Don't want old Mum cramping your style, do you? I'll be in the kitchen. You just call if you need anything,' she said, tucking two pillows behind Amber's back. 'And, Francis, our home is your home. You just make yourself comfortable.'

Once Colette was in the kitchen and the radio had been turned on Amber sat up and leaned close to me, pulling my face towards hers and kissing me hard.

'Thanks for coming,' she said, slumping back down.

'Thanks for having me,' I said back.

'No bother, mate,' she said, turning on the television. 'Do you want a drink? Tea? Coffee?'

'Whatever's easiest.'

'To be honest they're both a hassle so you might as well have what you like.'

'Tea then, I suppose.'

'Tea it is,' she said, before yelling our orders through to Colette.

We watched *The Apartment* again and it was just as good as it had been the first time.

'Have you watched the other films I was telling you about?' Amber asked as we sprawled together on the couch.

'No. Chris made me watch *Titanic* yesterday.'

'What is wrong with that man?'

'I know. He's the worst. Why do you only watch old films anyway? I mean, I like them, now you've told me to, but who made you like them?'

'Nobody *made* me like them. I just do. Dad used to put them on for us to watch after Sunday lunch.'

'Is that why you like them?' I asked, and Amber shrugged.

'I'd have liked to have met your dad,' I said.

There was a long pause while she looked at me blankly. I was worried I had upset her. It was like seeing a child fall over and that pained second when you can't work out if it's going to cry or not.

'He'd have hated you,' she said eventually, and then smiled.

'Why?'

'He'd have bashed you with his Union newsletter and made a speech about the evils of private education. And he'd have told you to get a haircut.'

'I'm bald,' I said.

'I'm working on the Dad not being dead and us not having cancer tangent. Feel free to join me at any point.'

'I'm fine where I am.'

'Coward,' she said, kissing my cheek. 'He'd have loved your mum, though. She might have won him round in the end.'

'She has her uses,' I said, going to get Amber the present from the mantelpiece. 'Here, open it.'

Amber didn't need telling twice. She unravelled the gift in one swift movement, like the opposite of origami, and it fell on to her lap.

'Why would you want *that?*' I asked, pointing at the manicure set. 'She's already given you the nail polish. I don't think she's taken enough time to get to know you,' I said apologetically. But Amber wasn't listening. She went quiet and smiled, holding on to the small set like it was treasure.

'I love it,' she said, placing it carefully on the coffee table. 'We should get everyone A-star Christmas presents this year,' she said after some thought. 'You know, to say thanks and sorry and everything.'

'We should. But what?'

'Mum's got a pottery wheel if you want to make people vases and stuff?'

I tried to explain that this wouldn't cut the mustard with Mum. I once made her a birthday fruit bowl in Art and she used it as an ashtray. When I corrected her as to its purpose she said that tobacco was a plant, but I knew she was lying because she looked dead guilty and the next day she'd washed it out and draped a bunch of grapes across the top.

'Are you a man of means then, Frankie?'

I told her no, keeping my secret savings account to myself. Something told me Amber was not the Rainy Day kind of girl, and would be as easily inclined to frivolous spending as a Pools winner or similar.

'Then it looks like the A-Team are going to have to come up with a plan,' she said.

The day was freezing but sunny, which was my favourite kind of weather. We'd gone outside to get some air when the tropical fug of the house had gotten too much.

Even though Amber's street was a bit scary and her whole house looked like it had been filled with the contents of a charity shop, Colette's garden was the sort that would win prizes. It was in bloom even in wintertime. Flanking the lawn, right down to the greenhouse, were beds of flowers and shrubs, and Amber knew the name of each and every one, sometimes in Latin. She told me about the snowdrops that would blossom even through ice; about the witch hazel that stayed green no matter what the season. She showed me the hellebores — beautiful but poisonous — and led me into the greenhouse where rhubarb grew, kept in the dark so that it was forced to grow more quickly, stretching up in search of the light. She told me that if you listened carefully enough you could hear it grow.

I took the hint and held my ear against the black plastic sheet while I nodded, smiling, neither confirming nor denying the phenomenon, the way you do when a pregnant woman pushes your hand towards her stomach and tells you to feel the kick inside. Amber talked about the plants the way she never did about people. The way she never did about anything else, really. It was as if she truly cared but for once wasn't scared to admit it, and didn't have to ice every sentence with a snide comment so that you'd no idea what she really meant.

'It's lovely,' I told her as we walked back inside.

'It's my favourite place in the world,' she said, taking her boots off at the kitchen door. 'Do you want to see my bedroom?'

It felt strange being in Amber's house. Being in her world. Hearing her talk about things she had done with her dad. About things her mum had taught her when she was a little girl, tottering around the garden with a watering can. It was sometimes hard to remember that she hadn't burst fully formed, like her own little universe, out of some cosmic explosion. That she had ever been taught anything, ever been looked after and raised into what she had become. That she had ever had a beginning.

She was different, too, in her own surroundings. Sometimes softer. Sometimes quieter. Sometimes it reminded me of the first and only time I had seen her cry. When I was at her house I loved Amber more than I had ever loved her before.

I suppose being in her house reminded me that she was human.

★ ★ ★

Up in her room Amber put on the first song of an album we had discussed at length on the unit, and started toying with the jewellery and ornaments that covered the top of her chest of drawers. On the windowsill a stack of papers and mementos, along with the card I had given her, were tied up with brown string after she'd been made to take them off the wall above her bed on the unit.

'Did it take long?' I asked.

'No. Don't know why they bothered making me anyway. I'll be back in before the week-end.'

'Don't say that.'

Amber shrugged and turned the music up.

'Did you like the garden?'

I told her I loved it, and that I loved hearing her talk about it even more.

When I said this she gave me a look she had never given me before. It was sort of the way Mum looks when she sees babies, flavoured slightly with the way Chris looks when he stares at certain boys in the record shops he always drags me to on a Saturday morning.

'Are you cold?' Amber asked. I said no. Slowly she moved towards me and took off her top. She kissed me, then began to unbutton my duffel coat.

'What time's your mum coming?'

'Five,' I said, as quickly as I could. If there was one thing I could have done without at that moment it was the thought of Mum's whereabouts.

'I'm pleased you're here,' Amber said, kissing me again, bending down as I sat back on the bed.

'I'm pleased you're back,' I told her, trying my hardest not to tremble.

'I do love you, Francis,' she said, as she pressed herself closer to me. 'I'm just not very good at saying it.'

*   *   *

We must have both nodded off because when I woke up Amber looked as bleary-eyed as I felt.

She let out a small laugh and moved up to kiss me on the lips. I held my arm around her, pleased that everything seemed to have stayed the same.

'Do you feel different?' I asked. 'You know, like anything's changed, since . . . *before?*'

She laughed slightly and sat up in bed,

reaching down to the floor to grab her jumper that had crumpled itself into a heap inside the crotch of my jeans.

'I feel *thirstier* than I did before. Do you want a drink?'

I said yes just as the last song reached its final bars.

'OK then, but get ready. Your mum's going to be here soon.'

Just as she was about to stand up the door handle turned and then opened.

'CHRIST!' Amber said, grabbing her jumper across her chest and standing up, perhaps quicker than any human has ever moved before.

I spun around in the bed and pressed my face into the pillows, assuming that if the worst came to the worst I could smother myself to death before the inevitable backlash and court case.

Fortunately it wasn't as bad as it could have been.

'Oh,' Olivia said, quizzically.

'Jesus, I thought you were Mum,' I heard Amber say, though didn't dare move from my pillowed den of shame.

'She's in the kitchen practising her singing.'

'Good. Don't say anything, Olivia. I mean it.'

'I won't,' she said. 'Were you . . . *experimenting?*'

I groaned into the pillow, praying for the sweet release of death.

'Olivia, seriously, just leave it. I'll talk to you later.'

'There are things you should bear in mind,' Olivia said. 'I saw a documentary. You have to be careful . . . '

'OL!' Amber yelled.

'I know, but are you aware of a film called *Juno?*' her sister asked.

At this Amber pulled a pillow from beneath my face, despite my best attempts to hold on for dear life, and threw it against the door.

'GET OUT!' she hissed.

'All right. But we can have that discussion later.'

'Yes,' Amber said, more calmly than before. 'Yes, we can. But please, Ol, give us a minute.'

I heard the door click shut, and Amber breathed out a long sigh of relief.

'You can come out, *stud,*' she said eventually, stroking her hand up my back.

'I think I'll probably just stay here for the next few years,' I said through the suffocating down of the pillows.

'If you think that's bad, your mum's just pulled on to the front drive,' she said, leaning over me to look out of the window.

I was up and dressed before Mum had even had a chance to lock the car door.

'How was meeting the Fockers?' Chris asked when we got back to the house.

'It was the best day of my life,' I said eventually, picking at some leftover stew straight from the pan.

'Well, something's put a smile on your face.'

I said nothing. I would tell him, eventually. I had no one else to confide in, and even if I did I'd want to tell my brother anyway. But at that stage I still wanted it to be a secret, something that only Amber and I knew, something that was special and ours.

Mum asked if I wanted something proper heating up but I declined. Really I just wanted to be alone. I took myself to bed and sent a text to Amber. For some reason I had been worried that she might no longer be sure about us. Like the time I'd spent all year desperate for the Blue Peter Tracy Island. I'd waited for what felt like an eternity as Mum spent every spare hour gluing egg boxes to tissue holders and pounding her old copies of *Vogue* into sloppy gloop from which she crafted mountains, like some snarling god who snapped every time someone came into the kitchen as she reached a pivotal stage with a pipe cleaner. Then, when the big day came, there was a brief thrill before boredom prevailed, and I went back to playing with my old favourites while the once-proud Tracy Island stood abandoned and desolate, like a ghost town, in the corner of my room.

Fortunately it wasn't the case as within minutes Amber had texted me back, saying that she was having a similar early night, in what I assumed would be an attempt to have extra-long dreams about her beloved (me).

I put on the same CD we had listened to in her bedroom and closed my eyes.

★   ★   ★

That night sleep must have happened like a blink-and-you'll-miss-it cameo, as when I opened my eyes after what felt like nothing but a brief nap it was morning. It was gone ten by the time I woke and when I went downstairs Mum was already in the kitchen, her files and notes spread out on the desk as she hammered away on her laptop like a piano virtuoso trying to bash the keys into her intended tune.

We ate breakfast in silence and I made sure to send Amber a text to let her know I was awake. She did not respond. For hours I cradled my phone like an injured pet, hoping that it would suddenly spark back to life with the familiar pip of a ringtone, or the oddly lifelike burr of its three brief vibrations each time a message came through.

Only there were no signs of life.

I waited all afternoon.

'A watched pot never boils,' Mum said as she fussed around the kitchen preparing tea. I ignored her and tried to will Amber through telepathy to respond. But still nothing.

After dinner (which I barely touched from worry and nausea) the phone rang. Mum answered and eventually came back into the kitchen looking serious.

Amber was back on the unit.

11

For a while she was on and off the unit on an almost daily basis.

'I'm like the damn mascot!' she'd spit when, once more, Colette had rushed her by midnight taxi back to the bed where she seemed to have been transplanted.

The one secret I ever kept from Amber was that on the night, after dinner, when Mum told me she'd been taken back to the unit for the first of many occasions, I was relieved. Relieved that my messages had gone unanswered not through lack of love, or — worse — waning interest, but due to her ill health and nothing more sinister.

I still feel a knot in my stomach when I remember how happy that news made me.

It was only when Amber was given time away from the unit that the difficulties in our relationship became apparent.

For one thing we lived miles apart, so either I'd have to take a bus (not really an option) or Mum would have to drop me off and face being held captive by Colette for 'bonding'.

That was the easy bit, though. The real

difficulty came with coordinating our Good Days so that they might occasionally overlap and we would actually get to see one another.

Some days I'd be physically unable to leave my bed; the pain would press down on me like a wrestler pinning my shoulders to the mattress. Only I was being pinned from inside, and nothing I did could shake its grasp.

On these days the buzz of my mobile would serve as my conscience, echoing through my room like a chime of regret as I groaned and writhed under the covers.

Then there would be days when I simply didn't want to get up. When the unfairness of everything seemed so vast all I could do was sit and sulk, glowering at the television as Mum came in and brought soup that I wouldn't eat and asked questions that I wouldn't answer.

On these days I would turn off my phone so that I knew all texts would be swallowed into the great abyss, and all attempts at calling would be met with the steely denial of the answer-phone message.

The last thing I needed on days like this was to see someone else as bald and miserable as I was.

Then of course there would be days when I'd feel good and well, and the thought of Amber made me rise early like the smell of frying bacon.

But unfortunately life isn't clockwork, and more often than not these would be the days when she would be bedbound, either laid up in agony or furious and miserable, and it would be my turn to fire off unanswered messages.

Sometimes I'd get so frustrated with hearing her answerphone that I was forced to call Chris at work to relay my woes.

'I don't know why she won't just text me back. Even a nasty one, so I know she's been getting them. Maybe my phone's broken . . . do you think Mum would get me a BlackBerry?' I'd suggest desperately.

'Your phone's not broken, Frankie.'

'Then why doesn't Amber text back? She could dictate to Colette who could transcribe the message and press send if it's too much effort. She's really not thinking of my feelings at all.'

'Cut her some slack. She didn't text back for the same reason you didn't. Don't be a dick, Francis, it doesn't suit you. If you're that desperate just use the internet like everyone else . . . ' Chris would say, laughing. It was usually around this stage I'd hang up on him too. If even he couldn't acknowledge the seriousness of my misery then it was a path I'd have to tread alone.

★　★　★

211

One morning, when we were unusually synchronised on our Good Days, Mum had agreed to drop me at the bottom of Amber's street. It suited us both fine that way. For me it meant Mum wouldn't launch into her monologue about how if she hadn't worked so hard Chris and I would have grown up somewhere like this, and how we would have made her a grandma before she was forty, and how we wouldn't be able so much as to spell Disneyland . . .

For Mum it meant she didn't have to go inside and have a cup of something herbal with Colette while she pretended to care about the plight of tribes in countries whose names sounded suspiciously unfamiliar.

'Are you wrapped up?' Mum asked, tucking my scarf inside my coat.

I said yes and pulled away. It had taken me more than ten minutes to get the scarf to lie the way I had intended. The overall effect was worth the effort. I cut quite a dashing image from the neck down.

'And you've got your mobile in case you need anything?'

'*Yes, I know, you're only ever ten minutes away* . . . ' I said, getting out of the car.

'And make sure you stay at Amber's. Don't go messing on outside.'

'I won't.'

'And if the house is too cold, make Colette put the heating on. Tell her I'll pay her bills for this quarter if I have to. I don't want you catching a chill.'

'Fine.'

'Just be careful, love, watch how you go,' Mum said as I slammed the car door shut in case someone heard her. The youths who clustered around Amber's house were somewhat unrelenting. She said she once saw a gang of them throwing rocks at a hedgehog. I wouldn't have stood a chance in the face of such menace, given my paltry immune system.

In truth, though, I had come to enjoy walking the length of the street towards her house. At first it had seemed ugly and scary. A girl had yelled 'Uncle Fester' at me, pointing at my bald head, the first time I'd ventured there, and I had been forced to increase my pace to a subtle canter in case the provocation became physical.

But already it was becoming second nature to me. I liked the abandoned playground with its layer of dry leaves and shattered glass. The image had even inspired the first stanza of what was looking to be a reasonably ambitious poem. And I liked the way some of the cars still had *Come on England!* flags stuck to their aerials; an act that seemed both sweet and aggressive at the same time. Also there never seemed to be any adults on the street where she lived, just feral children drinking out of big green bottles and glaring out from under greased fringes, like an amdram production of *Lord of the Flies*.

Mostly I liked the way being here made me feel. When I walked to Amber's house I imagined that I lived there, and that I would spend the whole night penning songs about escaping the grey streets to live a life of bohemian glamour. Amber's street always made you feel like you were in a Morrissey video. I hate Morrissey. So does Chris. But even we concede that his quiff is exemplary and worthy of imitation.

'How long are you back for?' I asked as Amber led me through the kitchen.

In the far corner of the living room a sorry-looking garden shrub had been adorned with fairy lights and tinsel. Colette thought it unkind to cut down trees for Christmas, and plastic was the heroin of the earth, so Amber and Olivia had been left to improvise.

'Don't know. Couple of days maybe. I'm sort of like a rock star in that respect. Almost every morning I wake up in a different postcode.'

'It's only different by two numbers,' I said.

'Still, it's a bit rock and roll.' She drained a carton of orange squash and crushed the empty box in her hands. She offered me a drink but I declined. She had texted me there on urgent business, which I had hoped meant a repetition of last time. Unfortunately it was not to be.

'I know you want to get everyone ace presents this year,' she began. I was crestfallen but put on a brave face nonetheless. In truth I was just happy to see her away from the unit.

'I suppose. I could empty my savings account. But I might need to give a week's notice for a large withdrawal.'

Amber shook her head and moved closer to me.

'I've got a better idea. You're going to love this,' she said, even though something about the look in her eyes told me the opposite was true.

'Is that a new coat?' she asked. I said yes. Mum had given it to me as an early Christmas present. I had described to her in detail the coat I had in mind for winter that year, and all credit to her she had listened for once and purchased accordingly. It was almost exactly the cut I had envisioned, though in all honesty I had been hoping for a slightly more pronounced lapel.

'Perfect,' Amber said, digging her hand deep into one pocket of it, then deeper into the other one, causing all manner of stirrings in the meantime.

'Frankie, you're packing some serious dollar,' she said, pulling out a fifty-pence piece.

'It's from Grandma. She says it's good luck to put money in a new pocket, but I think she's really just looking for ways to avoid Inheritance Tax.'

'Well, *there's that*,' Amber said.

'It might be true,' I said, suddenly defensive of Grandma's ritual, and keen not to buck a trend that left me at least a pound better off each year. Amber rolled her eyes. '*Oh, but it makes perfect sense to put crystals on your belly and hope it cures cancer*,' I said. She laughed and so did I.

'Careful, Francis,' she said, putting her hand back inside my pocket. I looked up at the flickering light bulb on the ceiling, trying to banish all impure thoughts from my head (of which there were many). 'You're even starting to sound like me,' Amber said, tightening her grip as she found what she was looking for. 'Don't want people saying I'm a bad influence, now do we?'

From my pocket she pulled out a plastic envelope with two spare buttons inside it.

'Bingo!'

'What do you need that for?' I asked, as she pulled out the buttons and handed them to me.

'All in good time, my dearest,' she said,

going over to the windowsill beside the table and taking down a box that was red and purple and decorated with all sorts of feathers and beads. If Colette were ever a box, this was the box she would be.

I couldn't see inside at first, but Amber seemed reasonably familiar with its contents.

'Here,' she said, pulling the box to the edge of the table so that I could have a closer look, 'guaranteed profit.'

Inside was a green mess that looked like dried grass cuttings. My first impression was not far from the truth. As the reality of the situation dawned on me I felt my knees weaken beneath me but was determined to save face in front of Amber.

She stuffed the button bag until it was bulging like an expensive pillow then handed it to me. I coughed and stuttered as I tried to prevent my entire body from shaking.

'It's weed, Francis,' she said matter-of-factly.

'I know.' As I spoke my voice rose sharply, like I was being nipped in the most delicate of areas. 'So . . . ' I tried to sound relaxed ' . . . your mum's OK with this sort of thing?'

'This *is* my mum's sort of thing. Herbal and organic . . . double whammy. She's just celebrating the earth's bounty or something.'

'Right,' I said. 'So she won't have a

Christmas tree but she'll dehydrate and burn a leaf until it's turned to ash?'

Amber shrugged.

'There's logic there somewhere, but either way it is what it is. Hand me that jar from the spice rack,' she said. 'The sage.'

I did as instructed and she sprinkled some of the herb into the box.

'What?' she said, as I looked on bemused. 'You've never topped up the vodka with water after you took a sip?'

I didn't dare tell her that I was seldom given the chance. Mum was neither glass half-full nor glass half-empty. She tended to order by the bottle.

'How are we going to go about this?' I asked.

'Dunno,' Amber said. 'We'll just hang around town. There're bound to be some anxious-looking hipsters trying to catch the eye of a potential supplier.'

The word she was looking for was 'dealer'. Someone who dealed. The sort of thing that people go to jail for. The sort of thing they make films about.

'Cool,' I said.

'You're going to have to take it. My jeans pockets are too small. It'll look obvious,' Amber said, pulling on a long coat that did conveniently seem to be entirely without carrying compartments.

I nodded and put the small package into the pocket of my new coat. It felt like a lead weight that was going to drag my whole body down towards the ground, so that everybody would see me walking, shamed and hanging, and simply know I was up to no good. I would be described as a scourge by the local press. I would never get into university. My first book would be memoirs of my time in prison.

The scandal would probably kill Grandma.

As she locked the front door Amber looked down at the ground and took a sharp intake of breath, like she'd just missed a really important penalty.

'Are you OK?' I asked.

'Yeah,' she said, leaning against the door, 'baby's just kicking.'

'We should go back inside,' I said, at least seventy per cent because I was concerned for her welfare. In truth even I wasn't feeling too spectacular.

'No,' she said, taking my hand and straightening up. 'I'm fine. I'll be fine.'

'I really don't think . . . '

'Francis! Know when to quit. We're going into town whether you like it or not . . . *bitch gotta make rent*,' she said, and kissed my cheek.

* * *

'I can't do this, Amber!' I said halfway down the street. I had counted one hundred and seventy-two steps in the time it had taken me to build up the courage to say as much.

'What you chatting about?' she said as we came to a stop outside the Metro station.

'This. It's all so wrong. It's going to end badly.'

'Positive mental attitude, Frankie. *Were Christian's teachings entirely lost on you?*'

'But we're MULES!' I said, and Amber fell about laughing.

I told her it wasn't funny. That entire motion pictures had been made about the terrible ordeals that befell people like us, and how someone had lost an ear in *Midnight Express*. I carried on talking until I stopped making sense even to myself and had to draw a huge deep breath like I had just surfaced after touching the floor at the deep end.

'Are you done?' Amber asked sarcastically, not at all befitting the dramatic nature of my speech.

'Yeah, and I want to go home.'

She moved closer to me and slipped her hands inside the pockets of my coat on both sides, kissing me on the lips as she did it.

'Francis, it'll be fine. It's just a bit of weed.

And you said it yourself — it'd be one hundred percent super-fly of us to get everyone surprise presents this year. We'd be, you know, hailed as saints for being so benevolent.'

'I suppose,' I said. 'But I still don't like it.'

'It's a tough life for a pimp.'

'I think I'm just too darn tired of husslin',' I said. Amber smiled.

'*Shut up and deal*,' she said, as she led me by the hand towards the Metro platform.

We sped along the tracks in near-silence. At first Amber tried to initiate conversation about what I wanted to buy Mum and Chris. I muttered something about having a look on the internet and then fell mute when the pressure of our self-imposed task proved too much.

Two stops before town Amber slid her hand into mine and started clearing her throat. I felt my whole body tense in response, assuming it to be some sort of drug dealer's code alerting me to the prospect that we would have to smash through the windows of the speeding train and flee the authorities. But when I looked around no one was there, just Amber, grimacing and coughing gently, like she was trying to bring up whatever was paining her.

'We can go back, you know,' I said. 'We can

still do it . . . I don't mind. But another day. You don't look well.'

'You're hardly the image of health yourself,' she said, squeezing my hand tighter and forcing a smile. 'I'm fine. Just being stupid.'

'If you're sure? Because if Mum finds out I've left yours, she'll kill us both.'

'I'll take my chances,' Amber said, and bumped her body against mine.

The train pulled into the last stop before town and we started to relax a bit. Through the gaps in the trees a sharp winter sun started to cut through the Metro carriage, making everything look golden and warm even though my hands were so cold that they had started to sting.

Neither of us saw them get on. Amber's hand rested gently in mine and I was staring at the floor. Trying to unstick a wad of Orbit from the sole of my shoe was taking up most of my attention. Just as the ugly clot of gum began to give way I felt Amber stiffen beside me. Then I heard a bark. Then another one.

The presence of a disgruntled canine would have filled me with dread at the best of times. I once started walking along a reasonably busy B-road to avoid an approaching Dalmatian. But even this primal fear was overridden when I looked up and saw them both — a man and a woman in uniform

— coming towards us. The woman was younger, maybe Chris's age. The man could have been someone's dad, only the closer he got the less of a paternal aura he seemed to give off. The dog carried on barking and the female police officer held on to its collar once she'd managed to gauge the direction of its interest.

'*Abort mission*,' Amber hissed under her breath.

'*What do I do?*' I said back, trying not to move my mouth.

'Just . . . be . . . cool,' Amber said as the police officers came towards us.

'Afternoon, you two, shouldn't you be in school?'

I looked to the floor. Amber didn't. She stared straight up at him, making sure to lock him in her gaze even though I knew the sun would be hurting her eyes.

'We're not at school. We're off sick.'

'Metro's no place for recuperation.' The policeman laughed, moving closer. 'Do you know what Toby over there is?'

'An unfortunately named woman?' Amber said, nodding towards the policewoman. I looked up and the policeman smiled but shook his head. 'Or do you mean your rubbish guide dog?' she tried again. The whole time the officer kept shaking his head.

'I think you know exactly what I mean, flower. Now are you going to make this easy or hard?'

'Easy,' I said.

Amber turned and glared at me.

'Right. Who's going to empty their pockets first?' he asked.

Eventually Amber moaned and shoved her hands into the one narrow coin pocket on the hip of her jeans. She pulled out a packet of cola-flavoured bubble gum and a losing scratch card.

'Very good. And now you, good sir,' the policeman said to me.

My hands were shaking so hard that at first I couldn't control them. Bravely I managed to demonstrate the pristine nature of my inside pockets, retrieving only the two spare buttons and a receipt from Fenwick's that Mum had left in so I'd remember how much the coat had cost and would be sure to take care of it. I went into my front left pocket then my front right, finally removing my hands.

'That everything?' the policeman said.

I nodded at first, but the dog was howling and moaning in the background and I feared that refusal to co-operate would result in a state-sanctioned mauling, so eventually I relented and pulled out the small bag of weed.

'Well, well, well,' the policeman said, taking

the bag from me. 'The plot thickens.'

'It's medicinal,' Amber said.

'It always is, pet,' the policeman said, shaking the small bag at the policewoman who rolled her eyes and took a treat from her pocket to feed to the hound, which silenced him momentarily.

'We've got cancer,' Amber announced.

The policeman looked flustered but then checked himself and resumed his dour expression.

'That may be, but the law's the law. And I'm afraid there's no such thing as a get-out-of-jail-free card. Now, what are your names?' he said, taking a pad from his pocket.

Neither of us spoke and the silence overwhelmed me, so eventually I cut in.

'Francis Wootton,' I said, and Amber groaned. 'Francis spelled with an *i*. I live at 111 Melrose Gardens . . . '

'All right, all right, I get the gist, kidder. And the lady?' he asked.

Silence.

I made a whimpering sound as Amber stood her ground and stared the policeman straight in the eye. Eventually she gave in.

'Amber,' she said.

'There a second half to that story?'

'Spratt,' she said. It was not the prettiest name at the best of times. But Amber always managed to make it sound like a swear word.

'Very good. Now I think you both know you're going to have to come back to the station with us.'

'Nooooooo,' Amber whined.

'Afraid so, love. We've to make you watch a video now so you won't do it again.'

'Come on, cut us some slack.'

'Doesn't work like that, darling,' he said. 'We'll call your parents . . . '

I heard this part then everything seemed to go mute for a moment. I had not even contemplated the possibility of Mum becoming involved in all this.

'Is there any chance I can ring my brother instead?' I asked. 'He's a responsible adult . . . '

'Is he your legal guardian?'

'He picks me up from school sometimes.'

'Sorry, lad, you're going to have to face the music, I'm afraid. We'll get in touch with your mam, don't you worry.'

I looked at Amber with desperate, frenzied eyes. She didn't seem scared, more indignant. She must have picked up on my terror, though, because she made one last-ditch attempt to plead mitigating circumstances and suddenly went limp, like her skeleton had been removed.

'*Oooooh, my cancer,*' she groaned, looking pained and weak.

She flopped sideways against me, and let her head fall against my shoulder as though she had passed out.

She didn't move. I looked at the policeman and he shook his head.

'Come on, love, don't play silly beggars.'

Amber still didn't respond. Her routine had failed in the most spectacular fashion but she deserved credit for persistence if nothing else.

'Amber . . . ' I said. 'Amber! Get up.'

'Mmmmmmm,' she said, rolling her head on my shoulder.

I looked first at the policeman and then the policewoman, busy feeding the gigantic hound treats from her pocket, before finally returning to the policeman who was growing ever wearier of Amber's dramatics. There was nothing else to say. I felt my entire life come crashing down around me and there was only one thing I could think of to do.

I leaned forward and threw up on his shoes.

12

Being at the police station was the single most terrifying forty-five minutes of my life. They registered us at a front desk, and then took us into two separate rooms. They offered me a drink but I declined, fearing truth serum or something that might render me unconscious. Two police officers came in and chatted together for a while and then left me to stew.

I didn't have time to worry about Amber. I assumed she would fare well in jail whereas I probably wasn't so well suited to life behind bars. I wouldn't last long. My dietary requirements, for one, would no doubt be ignored. Likewise my inability to sleep on sheets that had been washed without fabric softener.

It didn't help that the policeman left to sit with me was not the chatty type. Once I was feeling a bit braver I attempted to engage him in conversation, but was met with one-word answers at best so just had to sit there in fear of whatever came next. And having seen *Slumdog Millionaire*, I knew all too well how authorities dealt with youths of unlikely intelligence.

Every ten minutes or so another policeman would pop his head round the door and provide updates on Mum's progress towards the station. I'm sure this was some small attempt to make me feel better. (I'd cried twice and thrown up once more since my incarceration.) But in truth it just made me feel worse. All I could assume was that the policeman reporting on her movements was not the one who had been responsible for calling Mum.

After what felt like a lifetime I heard noise erupt in the hall outside and a woman's voice howling all sorts of threats. I could hear Mum demanding to see her son, and informing a stuttering officer that if I suffered any relapse in my condition then she would sue him personally, Northumbria Police *and* Newcastle City Council, and she would win.

'Sounds like your time's up, big lad,' the policeman said to me from behind his copy of the *Daily Sport*.

Suddenly I was not so scared of jail any more.

Mum came inside the interview room and burst into tears. I did not. My time at Her Majesty's pleasure had hardened me somewhat so I just let her hug me, though I shivered when through tears she whispered that as soon as I was better she was going to smack me into the middle of next week.

'Do you know just how unwell he is?' she asked the policeman who had been looking after me.

'That's why I was sitting in here with him.'

'Medically trained, are you?'

'I've got two eyes and know the number of a good ambulance service,' the policeman said with a chuckle.

Mum did not laugh. She just grabbed me by the arm and yanked me to my feet.

'This is far from over,' she said as a policewoman led us out of the room and down the corridor.

We were taken into a small office where another policeman, this one in a suit, sat behind a desk.

'Francis Wootton . . .' he said slowly ' . . . and this must be Mam.' She was so busy fussing about inside her handbag for her car keys that she didn't notice the way the policeman was looking at her. 'You don't remember me, do you?' he asked her eventually.

'Excuse me?' Mum said, confused at first. Only once she looked properly at the policeman for the first time her face changed. *'You're kidding?'* she said glumly, like she'd just noticed a flat tyre.

'It's been a long time,' he said to her.

'Good to see you again, Dennis,' Mum

said. The policeman corrected her, telling her it was DS Bradshaw these days. Mum just scoffed at this, with a short, cruel laugh, 'If that's not irony I don't know what is! Look, is this going to take long?'

'It's good to see you again too, Julie.'

'It's Mrs Wootton,' she said, then for no reason whatsoever added, 'in name only. Subject to change.'

At this the policeman looked like he'd got five balls right on the Lottery and was waiting for lucky number six. Mum just looked like she wanted to kill someone.

'How you keeping?' he asked.

'I've got an absentee husband, my own parking space at a cancer unit, and a druggie for a son,' she said, slapping my leg. 'How do you think it's going?'

The policeman laughed.

'Well, you'll be on your way soon. Couple of forms to fill out, a video to watch . . . '

'What?'

'Just a little deterrent we use.'

'We'll rent *Trainspotting*,' Mum said. I smiled, but made sure not to laugh, though this subtlety was not lost on her, or on DS Bradshaw, who stared at me.

'Nothing funny about what happened today, young man. Riding without a ticket, carrying a Class-C substance, soiling a carriage.'

'Oh, bloody hell,' Mum said. She was obviously unaware of the extent of our crimes. 'What did you do?'

'I was sick,' I said.

Mum pressed her hand to my forehead and started cupping my glands.

'But you're OK now? You're feeling better? Do you need some medicine?'

'I'm fine,' I said, but weakly enough that she'd think I was just being brave.

'Mercedes, eh?' DS Bradshaw said, pointing at Mum's key ring. 'Must be doing something right.'

'I hotwire cars,' she said. At this he laughed and even Mum smirked. 'Look, I'm sorry. Any other time, Dennis, and I'd have loved a catch up, but I really do need to get my son home. Can we just skip to the good bits of the video?'

The policeman huffed and shook his head, making it look like he was doing us a huge favour.

'All right,' he said. 'But only because I know you, Julie, and if there's one thing I'm sure of it's that your boy won't be doing it again.'

'I won't. Ever.'

'Come on then,' he said, standing up. 'There are a couple of things we need to get sorted then you're free to go.'

I sat by the windows as Mum filled out

some forms at the front desk.

'OH, NO!' she yelled, pointing her pen at one paragraph in particular.

'It's just protocol. A fifty-pound fine for soiling a Metro carriage.'

'He's unwell,' she said to DS Bradshaw, leaning forward and baring her teeth.

'It has to be paid. And by the looks of it, you're hardly strapped for cash.'

'It's a point of principle.'

'You're the one who was so keen to leave.'

Mum looked around the room and then glared at me.

'He's fifteen,' she said, this time more softly, 'same age as I was when you last saw me, I reckon. Come on, Dennis.' Her tone was worrying amicable. 'You must remember, all those years ago? We were just kids . . . the fun we used to have,' she said, then left a long pause. 'I was fifteen and you were nineteen, remember?'

I felt queasy. This was worse than being arrested for drugs. Mum was trying to sex-blackmail a policeman. They were going to make a documentary about us for certain. With her as my moral guide it was no wonder I had spiralled into a hell of crime and narcotics. I was only surprised it hadn't happened sooner.

'Julie, Julie, Julie . . . you cannot be serious?'

He didn't seem angry when he said it, the way most people would be. For some reason he seemed to be enjoying the confrontation. I should have thrown up again on the floor, just to teach them both a lesson. 'What exactly are you suggesting?'

I looked up and saw Mum raise her eyebrows the way women do in films before the screen fades to black.

'*Drop the fine,*' she said, '*or I'll ruin your life.*'

DS Bradshaw threw back his head and laughed hard.

'Oh, you've not changed a bit. Not one little bit.'

He picked up the sheets of paper and stacked them together neatly.

'You know, most people would be arrested for the stunt you just tried to pull?'

'Most people wouldn't dare try,' she said.

'That's for damn sure.'

'So?'

'All right then,' he said. 'Just this once, I'll pull some strings.'

'You make sure you do,' Mum said, slinging her handbag across her chest like it was body armour as she turned to summon me.

'And you watch yourself, young man,' Bradshaw said to me as we left the station.

'Next time it'll be ten to fifteen years, no question.'

I laughed weakly and scurried outside after Mum.

'Oh, and Julie love, you owe me a drink.'

Mum laughed and turned back into the police station, even though I had taken her by the hand and was yanking her in the opposite direction.

'Don't push your luck, Dennis,' she said before I finally managed to drag her away.

The car ride home was deathly silent. I went to put on a CD but Mum put out her hand to stop me.

'You sit tight until we're home, sonny,' she said. 'Then you're really going to get it.'

'I'm so sorry,' I started. 'I think it's the pressure of the last year . . . '

'That'll not wash,' Mum said. 'Just belt up and keep your head down. This is so far from over it's not even funny, Francis.'

* * *

Fortunately for me, the threatened reprimand was softened by the presence of Chris and Fiona.

As Mum pulled on to our street something white was dangling from her bedroom window. When we drew closer it became

235

obvious that it was the old double sheet from the garage that she had used to cover the floor when she was decorating the downstairs bathroom.

'FREE THE TYNESIDE TWO' was painted on it in block capitals.

'I will kill that boy,' Mum said in a whisper as she yanked the handbrake so hard it made the entire car shake.

She slammed her door shut and sprinted into the house. I was left to make my own way inside.

'GET IT DOWN NOW!' I heard her scream from inside. As I made it out of the car I saw the sheet being whipped back through the bedroom window, and within seconds Fiona was sprinting out of the front door and down the street.

Chris tried to wade in a couple of times while Mum was tearing a strip off me, but even he knew when to quit so eventually he just hovered in the background, looking concerned. At first she started by grounding me indefinitely. I nodded my acceptance, even though it seemed pointless to me. Other than the odd Good Day at Amber's, the farthest I ever really went was to the toilet, and even that required two sit-downs and a motivational speech from the closest relative to hand. Then she took to the podium and let rip for nearly an hour. Mum skipped through subjects like a pro, segueing seamlessly from how she'd worked every hour God sent to make sure Chris and I had a better start in life than she'd had, to prospective universities for me, all the time touching on the themes of unemployment, homelessness, and even a bizarre aside about a documentary she had seen where a boy not much older than me had been executed in Thailand for just smelling a bit like weed.

I sat at the table, looking dead sorry and nodding where appropriate, trying to keep up with the speed of her logic. After a while the sound of her voice faded to a murmur, like background music, and I became transfixed by her impressive ability to multi-task. Without in any way losing the thread she managed to unload and reload the dish-washer, make both Chris and me a sandwich, and handed me a glass of water with three pills from the day-by-day medicine box she'd organised for all of my tablets and potions.

'Trite sentiment for an enabler,' Chris said as I gulped down the pills Mum was pushing into my mouth. She took my empty glass and rammed it into the overfull dishwasher.

'*Too soon*,' she said with a snarl.

'I am sorry. I don't know what else to say. We were doing it for you,' I pleaded.

'Let's not go down that road again, Francis.'

'For Christmas presents. We wanted to get everyone the best Christmas presents ever, to say how sorry we were for this year.'

Mum still looked unimpressed.

'I mean, honest to God, Francis, there isn't anything you couldn't have. There isn't anything I wouldn't let you do.'

'You wouldn't let me go to Glastonbury,' I said, a subject that still rankled.

'You were thirteen!'

'Zak's dad was chaperoning.'

'Zak's dad has a purple beard and lives in a yurt. He'd probably have sold you for drugs money, which brings us conveniently back to where we started, *smart arse*!'

'I'm sorry,' I said in despair. Mum looked like she was going to go off on one again but then softened a bit, and stroked my head.

'I know, love. And I know it's not like you, so let's just draw a line under it for now, eh? We'll sort something out when you're feeling better.'

'Just one more thing,' I said eventually, eager to make as much headway as I could during her brief bout of friendliness.

'What, Francis?'

'You know how I'm grounded?'

'Yes, Francis.'

'I mean, so long as I promise not to go anywhere else, can I still see Amber, given the circumstances?'

Chris looked at the floor and shook his head while Mum breathed out loudly through her nose and kicked the dishwasher door shut. No more was said on the subject and so, optimistically, I took this as a 'maybe'.

★ ★ ★

Speaking of Amber, the saga wasn't quite over yet.

'IT WASN'T HER FAULT!' I wailed as Mum collected her car keys and buttoned up her coat.

'We'll see about that,' she said, opening the door.

'PLEASE!' I begged.

She'd made me text Amber to make sure she had got home all right. Assuming that meant Colette was with her, Mum had decided now was as good a time as any to give them both a piece of her mind.

'Francis, I will be diplomatic to the letter, but this needs sorting,' she said, halfway out of the door.

'But you'll ruin everything!'

I pointed out that with each barbed comment from Mum we were being pushed closer and closer towards *Romeo and Juliet* territory. Mum scoffed at this as she closed the door, and muttered something about being as far removed in dignity as could be, which I think was in reference to Colette only ever doing her big shop at LIDL.

'She's going to ruin my life,' I told Chris while he selected a roster of soothing tracks and I sprawled on the couch. The drama of the day had been overwhelming, so I'd taken a blanket to the front room and was resting my nerves.

'It'll be fine. Somehow I think Amber's more than a fair match for Mum.'

'Not in this mood.'

'Don't worry. She always does this. Once she stops snarling she can be pretty reasonable.'

To cheer me up Chris got out his laptop and we started looking for Christmas presents that we could buy online. For Grandma we bought a catering-size pack of sugar sachets, a pinny with a picture of the Tyne Bridge on it, and a small bottle of Bailey's. For Colette he ordered a *Best of Bob Marley* CD, which he said was a funny joke that was perhaps better kept from Mum.

We spent what seemed like hours looking for a present for Amber. It was as if nothing had been invented that could articulate my love for £15 or less. I suggested an engagement ring and Chris said that if Amber didn't kill me then Mum would. I could see his point. Toiletries seemed crass and chocolates unlikely. And buying CDs for people is a minefield; invariably your selection says more about you than it does them.

Then, on the last website, just as we were starting to give up hope, the perfect present presented itself.

'THAT!' I said.

Chris said he wasn't sure but I ignored him and pressed Order anyway.

★   ★   ★

I woke to the noise of two women screaming at one another and sat bolt upright, assuming the fight between Mum and Colette had spanned postcodes.

'You were out for the count so I didn't want to wake you,' Grandma said, looking concerned. (Though not enough to turn the volume down to less than twenty-seven, or to avert her eyes from the TV.)

'I didn't know you were coming round,' I said.

'I wasn't. But I sat on my remote and lost ITV. I had to catch my programmes.'

Chris came through from the kitchen with

241

a pot of tea just as Mum's car pulled on to the drive.

'So it resumes,' he said, and Grandma shushed him.

I checked my phone and noticed several messages from Amber.

The first was all in block capitals and said that Mum was going to kill Colette. The second was to make sure I was OK and to say that she thought I would probably be asleep, so she wouldn't text again. The third one said everyone was friends again, and Colette had cried but in a good way, and that Amber hoped I didn't hate her for getting me arrested for selling drugs *(smiley face x x)*.

I texted her back so that she knew we were still in love, and then waited for Mum to come in shouting and bawling. Only she didn't. She just looked fed up and harassed.

'What's she doing here?' she said to Chris.

'Her telly's broke.'

'For God's sake! *You know they have plenty of working TVs in care homes?*' Mum said, but Grandma ignored her.

'How did it go?' I asked. Mum glared at me then pointed at Grandma.

'How did what go?' Grandma asked, still not looking at anyone.

'Mum went for a coffee at Colette's,' Chris said.

'Oh ... ' Grandma chuckled to herself ' ... sooner you than me.'

I asked Mum again how it had gone, and eventually she rolled her eyes and poured herself a cup of tea into the mug Chris had brought in especially for me. She could be really selfish at times.

'They're coming for Christmas,' Mum said with a sigh.

I beamed and went to hug her. Sometimes she could be the best person in the world, even if she did frown all the time.

'Oh, get off, you soft sod,' she said, pushing me off her.

The news had certainly been enough to snap Grandma away from her programmes.

'Oh, Julie, no,' she said, with a look of pure terror in her eyes. 'They're not normal. Besides, that's family time.'

'Yeah, well, I'm sure there'll be an obliging soup kitchen if you don't like it.'

Chris gave Mum a secret sort of nod that meant he approved of her actions, and Mum shook her head like she always does when she's the one who has to keep everything together (which is always, if truth be told).

'Right,' she said eventually, taking her cup of tea and a packet of cigarettes from the coffee table, 'I'm having the girls round tonight. I need a proper drink after the day

I've had. If anyone wants me I'll be in the conservatory. Do not disturb me unless it's urgent.'

Grandma still looked gutted but I couldn't bring myself to care. Amber and I were going to spend our first Christmas together. It was as though we were a family already. It wasn't without its worries, though. The tree would have to be perfect this year: colour blocked and symmetrical, like the one on the decorations box. And a single present for Amber wouldn't be enough. I would have to fill an entire stocking for her so that she knew how much I cared.

I opened the laptop straight back up and began to search for more things.

'Are you staying for tea?' I asked Chris.

'No, flower, I'll be getting back,' Grandma said, having returned her attention to the soap operas.

'Yeah, I'll stay,' Chris said, and gave a proud wink as he poured us both a cup of tea.

13

That night Mum stuck to her word and had the girls round.

Lisa and Lindsay appeared not long after tea with carrier bags full of wine and beer.

'Hiya, gorgeous,' they both said, kissing me when they found me in the kitchen.

I sat with them for a while. Mum was polite even though I knew she wanted me to go to bed so that she could be debauched. I stuck it out, though, being charming. It was a wise investment. As I made my way upstairs Lindsay necked her third glass of rosé and grabbed me to her bosom.

'You look after yourself, love,' she said. Not realising perhaps that if they weren't so keen on recreating Gin Lane in our conservatory then Mum might have been in a position to do just that. 'And this is from the both of us, for your Christmas box. Get yourself into town when you're feeling up to it.'

She pressed a £50 note into my fist.

Upstairs I folded it in half like an expensive shirt. I'd never seen one in real life before. It looked red and dramatic and almost so cartoonish it could have been a fake. I held it up to the light like a shop assistant, trying to spot signs of forgery, but wasn't entirely sure what I was looking for. I made a mental note to swap it for two twenties and a ten at the first given opportunity, lest my efforts had been in vain.

I didn't mind going to bed early, either. 'The girls' frightened me. I'd observed their behaviour from the landing at Mum's fortieth. As soon as they got on it they became quite inhuman. In conversation they would approach subjects the way a flock of pigeons might a tossed chip; flapping and cawing over one another until said subject was desiccated and of no use to anyone. They also didn't seem to realise that any bottle opened after one in the morning would result in a dramatic crying competition, like at a state funeral or a Beatles concert.

I tried to be as understanding as I could but all night I could hear them, pounding their feet to and from the fridge, slamming doors, glasses being smashed and Mum shrieking with laughter. I wanted her to have a nice night because of how good she'd been, but at half-twelve — three-quarters of an hour into the karaoke session — I was becoming frenzied with exhaustion and possibly also delirious.

I tried banging on the floor with my

lacrosse stick, to little avail. Then I made a moaning sound hoping that some maternal intuition would alert Mum, like Lassie had I fallen down a well.

Once more I was disappointed.

Eventually I sent her a text asking her to come upstairs.

Seconds after I'd pressed send the music went dead and there was a moment's blissful silence. I became quite giddy with authority and thought about sending another text — maybe a song request — just to see how much power I could wield at the push of a button. But then Mum came stumbling in. She had smudged mascara, one shoe missing and a feather boa around her neck. She looked like the 'before' picture in a rehab brochure.

'What is it?' she said, holding herself up in the doorway. 'Do you need your medicine? The nurse?'

'I can't sleep,' I said. 'It's too noisy.' Mum snorted with laughter then came to sit on my bed, making an unconvincing job of looking sympathetic and innocent all at once.

'Sorry, love,' she said, leaning awkwardly against my headboard. 'It's the girls. I can't keep control of them.'

She grabbed one end of her feather boa and teased it across my face.

This wasn't entirely fair. It was not their unique take on 'Bat Out of Hell' that had tipped me over the edge (too easily we forget that the song is within touching distance of the ten-minute mark).

'That's OK,' I said, pretending to be sleepier than I was. 'You deserve a night off.'

'Oh, darling . . . I never want a night off from you,' Mum said, and went to kiss me but ended up face-planting the pillow.

'I'll be fine,' she said, standing up and stroking her palm hard across my face so that my bottom lip stretched down to my chin.

Just as she was about to leave there was a ruckus on the stairs and the girls appeared in my doorway, looking like the Ghosts of Christmas Future. Or a frightening vision of what can happen if you approach middle age without due dignity. At their time of life they should be wearing trouser suits and baking cakes, maybe spending their days penning hand-written letters of complaint to newspapers. Not drinking alcopops with crude straws in them.

'Sorry, darling, we'll try to keep it down,' Lindsay said, shaking a bottle in one hand and trying to press one finger to her lips with the other.

'Are you missing your little girlfriend?' Lisa asked, to stifled amusement from the others.

'Here, handsome, you couldn't sort us out with some gear, could you?' Lindsay said, to full-blown hysterics.

'Come on . . . ' Mum said from the doorway ' . . . out.'

' . . . do you think we should give him a few tips?' I heard Lindsay murmur as Mum shut the bedroom door and left me in peace.

★ ★ ★

The morning after the whole house was deathly still. Mum had got up, made sure I was OK, then returned to bed with a big bag of crisps and a packet of Aspirin. She didn't resurface until gone twelve, which was negligent. I could have fallen and concussed myself, and she would have been none the wiser.

Fortunately Chris had come round to visit so I was not entirely without supervision. I'd tried showing him the empty bottles in the recycling bin but instead of looking horrified he'd been impressed. When it comes to drinking he and Mum share the self-restraint of Slimer from *Ghostbusters*, so I don't know why I was surprised.

Mum finally resurfaced just before lunch-time.

'Wrath of grapes?' Chris asked.

'You'd know,' she said, opening the letters that I'd fetched from the doormat. 'Bills . . . bills . . . bills,' she said, tossing the unopened envelopes on to the couch. 'Does anyone want any lunch?'

★   ★   ★

'We did it,' I said to Chris once we were alone, suddenly keen to share my secret.

'Who?'

'Me and Amber.'

'Oh,' Chris said. He looked at me like I'd picked up an instrument he'd never seen before and had started playing it like a virtuoso. 'Congratulations. Is that what we say?'

'I suppose. I was proud.'

'And everything went . . . '

'*Fine. Yes.*'

'Well, what do you know?' Chris said with a big grin. 'Frankie's a lad in all caps locks. GO ON, MY SON!' he said, pulling me into a hug.

Just then the doorbell rang.

'I'll get it then, shall I?' Mum hollered as she made her way through the back passage.

The door clicked open and there was a draught of cold air.

'*You have got to be kidding!*' I heard her

say, before the door slammed shut.

The bell rang a dozen more times before Mum answered it again. She came hurrying into the front room and turned off the video game Chris had been playing before he'd even had a chance to save it.

'Nice one,' he said, getting up to put the game back on.

'Sit down, love. Now,' she said.

Chris did as he was told as soon as we both saw how serious she looked. The doorbell kept ringing and a key rattled in the lock. A man's voice swore from outside when it wouldn't work.

'It's your dad,' Mum said. I felt a wave of nausea pass over me and Chris made a huge sighing sound.

'What does he want?'

'God knows. He's had long enough.'

'Just don't let him in. We can sneak out the back,' Chris said.

'Why?' I asked.

'The last thing you need is upsetting,' said Mum, tucking the credit-card bills behind a cushion. This didn't make much sense, though, as I seemed to be the only one in the room who wasn't in the slightest bit moved by Dad's appearance out of nowhere.

'Julie . . . Julie . . . don't be so stupid!' he yelled through the letterbox.

'I'm going to have to let him in. Just stop in here until I've had a word.'

'Well, I don't want to see him,' Chris said.

Mum nodded and went to open the door.

★　★　★

'What the hell do you think you're playing at?' Dad asked.

'Get inside. Now,' she said, slamming the door behind him.

'Is he here?'

'They both are.'

'Francis!' Dad yelled from the hallway.

I didn't answer. Chris started to look nervous and gave my leg a reassuring tap.

'It'll be OK,' I whispered. He nodded but didn't look convinced.

Dad came towards the front room but Mum stopped him dead in his tracks.

'I don't think so somehow,' she said.

'I remember the way. I'll get there before you do.'

'You have *no idea* what we've been through over the last six months . . . ' Mum hissed in the hallway, partly to scare Dad — which probably worked — and partly so we couldn't hear, which didn't. 'If you think you can just walk back in here and upset the apple cart, you've got another thing coming.'

'Give it a rest, Julie.'

'So help me God, Keith, if you upset either of those two lads I will kill you myself, do you understand?'

'Nice to see you've mellowed with age,' he said. Then Mum called him something so rude Chris choked on his Ribena and it came trickling out of his nose.

'I'm warning you. We'll talk about this later,' Mum said.

When Dad came into the living room I was shocked to see how old he looked. I think being an adulterer and an absentee father must have taken its toll on him. It was no wonder he and Mum went their separate ways. She was still reasonably well preserved for her age. He would have showed her up at business functions and wedding receptions. Even his suit looked creased.

'I'm in the kitchen if you need me,' she yelled, and Dad grimaced.

No one said anything. Chris had gone the opposite way to Dad. He looked like a little boy. An angry and sullen one, but a little boy nonetheless.

I think Dad had assumed there would be an emotional reunion. I think he'd pictured one of us crying. Maybe all of us. And then there would be hugs and apologies and promises that we'd never leave it so long again.

None of which happened. I wasn't angry. I wasn't sad. The only thing I felt was a nagging concern that, with all the drama, Mum's promise of lunch might have slipped her mind. That and the fact that for the first time in my life I felt as though it was I who should be looking after Chris.

'Hiya, lads,' Dad said, cautiously.

'Hello,' I said.

He made his way over to the settee and then sat down on the footstool, like he wasn't planning on staying for any length of time. I craned my neck to see if he had left a suitcase or a holdall in the hallway.

The fact that he hadn't made me relax a little.

'Chris,' he said.

'Right, I'm off.' My brother got up to go but I held on to his arm.

He looked at Dad, and then at me, and eventually sat back down, heavily, like he was being punished.

'Good of you to make it,' he said.

'I deserved that,' Dad said. 'I'd have come sooner, but . . . you know . . . *God, Frankie, you look terrible* . . . '

As icebreakers go it was pretty far off the mark. Besides, I felt I looked quite dapper that morning. Having watched the original *Ocean's Eleven* with Amber, I had been inspired to fashion a pocket square for my pyjamas that morning. The effect was lost on Dad who hadn't even done up the top button of his shirt. He really was unravelling.

'How are you feeling?' he asked.

Chris rolled his head back and sighed.

'Give it a rest, Christopher. This isn't easy on me either.'

'Been a tough few years, has it?' Chris asked. Dad looked like he'd been winded.

'I'm so sorry,' he said, getting up to hug me. I flinched, and Dad sat back down again. 'Sorry. Baby steps, eh? You're a young man now. Don't want hugs off your old dad.'

Eventually Chris did get up and leave me and Dad to it.

'I'm going to check on Mum. If you need me then just shout,' he told me.

★ ★ ★

The whole time Dad spoke I just stared at him blankly, thinking that if there was one person who would really be able to defuse this situation it was Amber.

I also started to think that I might like to tell Dad about her. Maybe see if he was impressed by how pretty and clever she was. Having not been to school lately, I couldn't wow him with accolades received for my intellect, like I would normally have done. And I was in no physical shape to impress him with, say, sit-ups or my annual Sports Day silver medal.

The more I thought about it, the more I thought that maybe he would like to hear about Amber. Maybe he'd have laughed. Or hugged me. Or gone to the pub and told all his friends that his son had his first girlfriend. I'd been forced to wing it up to that moment, but he might have been able to give me some advice.

But then again we'd done all right, winging it. And if I needed advice then there was Chris for that. And Mum. And to have given him the news about Amber would probably have made Dad happy. And he didn't deserve to be happy with us, because when we'd all been as miserable as we'd ever been he had left, kicking open the door to a whole new world of things for us to worry and cry about.

I felt my face shrivel into a scowl. Dad ruined things. It was what he did. He didn't fit in with the routine we'd had to build around him not being there any more. He didn't even seem to fit in with the living room properly. He looked at odds with the wallpaper and the furniture we'd changed since he'd been gone, like the giant packages we would take in for next door when they missed their delivery — packages that just got in the way no matter where we put them. Packages that belonged somewhere else. It was at that moment I decided that he wasn't getting Amber. And he wasn't getting me either.

'You do know I made what I felt was the best decision for us all at the time?' he said at one point, and suddenly I was glad that Chris wasn't still sitting with us. He could be quite confrontational at times. He'd interrupted conversations in restaurants before to explain to people why they were wrong.

'You and your brother, you were just . . . ' Dad went on, but I had let my mind wander. He kept screwing up his face as if he wanted me to help him out by saying the hardest bits for him. Or maybe tap him on the knee and wink, telling him it was all OK. I was not prepared to do this. Part of me enjoyed seeing him squirm, trying to gloss over his own behaviour.

The game was still spinning angrily in the console where Chris had left it. Dad started patting his jacket flat against his body, like he'd only just realised he'd forgotten to iron it. He really was a sorry sight.

'I brought you something for Christmas,' he said, eventually, reaching into his bag.

It was a card.

'Shall I open it now?'

'If you like.'

It was a Christmas card intended for a child, with a cartoon reindeer on the front. When I took it out of the envelope a misty avalanche of glitter cascaded across the blanket I had wrapped around myself. Only two things about the card were of interest to me. Firstly, there was no money inside. Secondly, that another woman's name soiled the page.

Wishing You a Merry Christmas and a Happy, Healthy New Year. With Love, Dad and Barbara, it said. There were two kisses beneath the writing. One of them I took to be from Barbara.

Dad was clearly out of the loop on matters of child rearing. And for a moment I felt the urge to dispense some valuable advice on such matters.

E.g. for the same reason my cancer diagnosis was not presented to me in a gift-wrapped box by a smiling stranger, so the name of the woman that you abandoned the family unit for should not be introduced via a Christmas card. Common sense ought to have told him as much. But then again, common sense clearly was not high on Dad's list of priorities.

I felt the foundations of our family shift an

inch or two, like a tiny earthquake had rippled beneath them. We were inching ever closer to the territory where differences are aired on late-morning chat shows.

'It would be nice if you could meet her one day,' Dad was saying.

I stared at him with the chilly indifference of a psychopath.

' . . . in time,' he added, and turned to face the TV even though it was on standby.

'Tell you the truth, I didn't know what to get you,' he said, but the card had done it for me. Suddenly I didn't even feel sorry for him any more. He was just another visitor to our house. One who had upset Mum and made Chris go all floppy and awkward. I wanted him gone, and I wanted him gone fast. But first there was the small matter of compensation.

'Just work out how much you would have spent and give me the equivalent in cash,' I said, taking control of the situation. It was the first full sentence I'd spoken the whole time he'd been sitting there. Dad had barely let me get a word in edgeways. He'd managed to talk solidly for nearly fifteen minutes, all the while saying nothing of any worth and leaving the important stuff written in biro on the back of a reindeer's face.

'Probably what you need at your age

. . . some money to go into town with. I'll write you a cheque,' he agreed.

'Cash would be better. There's a machine in the bottom shop now. You've got to pay one twenty-five to make a withdrawal so Mum won't use it because she says it's robbery. But you can just deduct that from the overall amount if you feel the same way.'

'Right,' Dad said, looking a bit flustered. 'If that's what you want.'

'And get exactly the same amount for Chris, too. Because I used all the coloured ink in his printer and he's saving for a car, so every penny counts at the moment.'

'Right.'

I yawned and hunkered down into my nest on the couch, feeling quite pleased with the way things had panned out. Though devoted to the arts, I sometimes think I could make quite a splash in the business world.

'You feeling tired?' Dad asked. I nodded and made my eyes go all heavy so that he'd get the point doubly fast.

'Well, you take care, kid. I'll sort out your Christmas box before I go.'

'And Chris's,' I said with my eyes closed as I heard Dad stand up and make his way out of the living room.

I must have method acted my way through my fake nap because when I woke up it was tea-time and he had gone.

'You look worn out,' Mum said when I joined her in the kitchen. I didn't say anything. My pocket square had fallen out while I was asleep and was lost for ever in the sea of blankets and old tissues that I had made my home for most of the day, so I probably did look quite unkempt.

'Well, I feel fine,' I said as she got up to put the kettle on. She came back and gave me a big hug from behind.

'Did Dad leave any money?' I asked Chris, who nodded and pointed to the sideboard.

'How many zeroes?'

'Two,' he said. '*Just.*'

While the lasagne was cooking Mum sent him upstairs to have a look at her laptop. I knew it wasn't really broken because I'd been playing on it the night before, so assumed this meant she wanted A Serious Talk.

'You all right?' she asked when we were alone.

I told her I was.

'You know, Francis, the one thing you do need to understand is that your dad left *me*. Not you.'

'It doesn't work like that, though. We sort of come as a package,' I said.

Mum laughed and stroked my face.

'You're a good boy. You both are. But I

made sure I got his new number. If you ever want to see him, you know, you've only got to ask.'

'I don't,' I said. Mum tried her hardest not to look relieved.

'I just don't ever want you to think you've got to do anything out of . . . oh, I don't know . . . *loyalty* to me. He's still your dad. He still loves you.'

'I know,' I said. 'But at the minute I prefer him from a distance.'

'Chris feels the same way, so I suppose that's settled. Now you look OK, so you can set the table for me. It'll be ready in fifteen minutes,' Mum said, making her way upstairs to tell Chris that it was all right for him to come down.

★   ★   ★

Mrs Babshaw from across the street had seen Dad coming into our house. She'd phoned her daughter to let her know, and her daughter had phoned her mother-in-law, who went to the same bowls club as Grandma. As a result Mum had to spend an hour after dinner on the phone to Grandma, dissuading her from making a guest appearance.

'It's sorted. The last thing we need today is another visitor,' Mum said, getting more frantic each time she had to stop Grandma from booking a taxi to come and stand guard against any more unannounced visits from ex-husbands.

'Did you show her the card?' I asked Chris when she'd left the room.

'She knows,' he said.

So did Chris, it turned out. Everyone in the world had known except for me. I could hear Mum in the hallway still ranting to Grandma.

' . . . *of course he was on his own. For God's sake, even he knows better than that!'*

Normally this was the sort of thing we kept from Grandma. Her generation cannot handle the complexities of modern love. To people of Grandma's age an affair is something as rare and confusing as an en suite; the sort of thing only film stars and foreigners have.

'Are you OK?' Chris asked me.

I said I was fine.

'Well,' he said, 'it's been a big month. You've dropped your V-plates and learned that your parents aren't as great as you thought they were. Welcome to Big School, mate.' He poured some of his beer into my lemonade so that it made a weak shandy.

'Mum's a bit great . . . ' I said, but quietly enough so that she wouldn't be able to hear ' . . . sometimes.'

Chris took another swig of beer and

thought for a second.

'I suppose,' he said, 'she can be a *bit* great
. . . *sometimes*.' He spoke even more quietly
than I had done just as Mum came back into
the kitchen, holding the phone like a gun.

'However bad things get, just remember
. . . they could always be worse,' she said,
referring to Grandma, then cocking the
phone as she slid it back into its holster. 'You
lads all right?' She was pouring some of
Chris's beer into her empty glass and taking a
big gulp.

'Yeah. How you doing?' he asked.

'You two don't have to worry about me.
I'm just fine. I've got my lads, I've got my
house, and I've got my mother on hold until
at least tomorrow,' Mum said with a smile.
She bashed her glass against Chris's and then
against mine, giving Chris a pretend look of
disapproval when she noticed the beer scum
tainting my lemonade.

'Cheers, boys,' she said. 'Here's to the best
Christmas yet!' And drained her drink.

14

Christmas got off to a slow start.

During the week leading up to the big day I had texted Amber twenty-eight times. She had responded seven times. This worked out as a ratio of 4:1 which I knew because Mum had started picking up schoolwork for me to do at home when I was feeling up to it. It was testament to Amber's lax input that I even had a spare moment in which to contemplate maths coursework.

On Christmas Eve morning Grandma went to turn on the bathroom light and the whole house was plunged into darkness.

She hollered for help but Mum just ignored her and told Chris to go and sort it out. I aimed the torch into the cupboard for him while he probed for the right fuse.

'I think it might be a sign that bad things are coming,' I said. 'Like a metaphor . . . '

'It's fine, Francis,' he said sharply.

' . . . and I saw a magpie on its own, outside my window. This means sorrow, in case you don't know. It's like the whole planet is heading towards certain doom . . . '

'Just hold the bloody torch still, Frankie.'

In fact, I had taken to superstition in a big way. Amber's condition had been on and off more than ever during the weeks leading up to Christmas, which I took to be the reason behind her waning commitment to our love. To remedy this, I became determined to do everything in my power to make her better from afar. Mum had got me some new trainers as another early present and I'd made sure not to put the box on the table while I opened them up. When Grandma came into the house I lunged at her. She thought it was for a hug, but really it was so that I could snap her umbrella shut before the universe noticed and doomed us to more bad luck. In the bathroom I'd open the cabinet as gently as if I were inspecting a child, lest the glass smash and grant us seven more terrible years. I wouldn't even walk into the conservatory, fearing that the gaps between the tiles held the same harmful power as cracked paving stones.

I was trying to explain all this to Chris when he let out a short scream. At first I thought it was from boredom. Sometimes my theories are beyond even him. But he seemed to be implying that he'd received an electric shock. I suspect this was a bid for attention because I'd got my new trainers and he was feeling left out, even if the howl of agony he emitted was particularly believable, like a musk-ox being mounted.

'There!' he said, angrily, as every light in the house flooded back on. 'You do know you're the most useless person in a disaster, Francis?'

★ ★ ★

'If they don't come I'm not getting out of bed on Christmas Day. You'll have to bring my presents and dinner to me in bed like I'm an elderly Royal,' I warned Mum as she carried on mulling every liquid to hand.

The Spratts had been pencilled in to arrive on Christmas Eve and spend the night, but Colette had just rung to say that she wanted Amber to get a good night's rest so they would make their way to us on Christmas morning. It seemed that Colette's cheery façade masked a soul of pure darkness, as not only did this break my heart, it also required a major re-draft of the Christmas Day Schedule I'd printed off and stuck to the fridge. I had considered every eventuality, and choreographed it to the letter. I'd even been sure to leave 'Subject To Change' gaps, which was code for 'getting off with one another while everyone else is busy'.

'Maybe best they don't come then. The

poor lass needs her rest . . . ' Grandma said, cutting crosses into the bottoms of Brussels sprouts. She was already in a bad mood. The night before Uncle Tommy had phoned her up at half-past nine to wish her a Merry Christmas. Whenever the phone rings after six o'clock at night Grandma assumes it is to inform her of a major disaster and clutches her rosary beads before answering.

Mum turned and glared at her and she shut straight up.

'I'm just saying, they've got their own house. And that funny mush you've had to get in . . . ' Grandma said, pointing to the nut roast Mum was doing for Colette.

'Well, it's happening so get used to it,' Mum said, turning up the radio with a smile as she grabbed hold of me and forced me to dance to the first bit of 'All I Want for Christmas is You'.

Chris had helped me to re-do the tree so it was perfect, only every time I looked at the box to make sure it was just like the picture, he'd wolf down another chocolate bauble and we'd have to start all over again.

'But I'm hungry!' he kept moaning. Chris does not understand the importance of love. Mum says his idea of long-term is staying for breakfast.

'We'll be done soon. Have a mince pie,' I

kept telling him while he adjusted the highest rung of lights so that they hung in three perfect lines.

Under the tree some of our lesser presents were displayed. I am naturally inquisitive, which is probably why I excel at Science, so poked my finger through a parcel with the cheapest-looking paper on it and caught a glimpse of something purple. Past experience informed me that this could only mean a selection box; the most thoughtless and hateful present of them all. A selection box is the wrapped equivalent of a shrug. You may as well not bother.

'Frankie, if you don't stop going at those presents like a crazed surgeon, I'm taking the whole tree down,' Chris said. His present to me was under there, too. I think he was keen not to ruin the surprise.

I apologised but explained that I was doing it for selfless reasons. The year before Grandma had got her labels mixed up, so that I'd ended up with a cat basket and one of her friends had my iPod speakers. She'd spent most of the morning crying and I'd had to lie and say that I'd always wanted a pet, so it was one step in the right direction, which just about perked her up. But then when she'd found out said friend had already returned the speakers to John Lewis for a store credit she went all weepy again.

'Shut up, Frankie,' said Chris, unwrapping another chocolate bauble.

★ ★ ★

'Well, Merry Christmas, you lot,' Mum said, raising her glass to us after tea while Chris and I both unwrapped our Christmas Eve present.

It was pyjamas. It was always pyjamas.

'At least you might actually wear them this year,' Mum said, pointing to me. I'd become quite used to wearing nothing but nightwear. Even when I visited Amber, I would just pull my jeans and jumper over whatever I had slept in. Quite apart from the cancer this was probably why I spent three-quarters of my day napping. I made a resolution to dress for success come the New Year. I'd have no choice but to anyway. Talk lately had been veering towards my returning to school for half-days.

'Oh, there's these as well. But there are conditions so don't get too excited,' Mum said, handing me and Chris an envelope each, inside which was a ticket to Glastonbury.

'Your brother's taking you . . . ' she told me as I hung from her neck like a pet monkey ' . . . and bringing you back. And you are to ring me every two hours otherwise I will drive down there myself and drag you back, do you understand?' I agreed whole-heartedly. Grandma didn't look so sure. I'd made her watch Glastonbury with me that year on television. It took three different acts on the pyramid stage and a flash of a BBC helicopter before she would believe it wasn't a documentary about the Somme.

★ ★ ★

'YOU CAN COME DOWN ... HE'S BEEN!' Mum yelled from the front room the next morning, after we'd opened our stockings in her bed.

'Pull the curtains, Julie, let the day in,' Grandma said while I tore through my presents.

'Let the fire warm the place up first,' Mum said, coming to sit by me on the sofa.

Chris always pretends he's not as excited by Christmas as I am, so he lets me open my presents first, but I could tell that each time I paused to glance at instructions or scan a blurb he was getting more and more riled.

Beside the fireplace, where the important family cards were displayed, a candle was lit. Next to the candle was an unopened card with Emma's name on it; and next to that, an unopened jewellery box wrapped with a red ribbon. Since I was six, this shrine would be laid out for Christmas Day, exactly the same each year. It would be gone by Boxing Day. Neither me nor Chris knew what happened to the offerings. We didn't ask.

Sometimes through the day if you passed the kitchen door when Mum was by herself, you could catch her talking to Em, too. Not full on conversations, just little things, like 'Merry Christmas, my lovely girl' she'd say, or 'I'll tell you one thing, you'd be glad you skipped this year'. Then, once, 'Oh shit, sweetheart I think I've left the giblet bag inside . . . '

Nobody ever interrupted. Nobody even acknowledged it. It was nice, in a way. It was Mum's way of keeping something going that made her happy. Some loves, like the one Mum felt for Dad, disappear for ever and are best forgotten about; some are best suspended in the amber of memory — localised to a specific time and place, like a really great dish you ate at a restaurant on holiday; and other loves carry on for ever, no matter how distant their nucleus becomes. Like Mum's love for Emma. It didn't matter that it didn't have anywhere to go any more; it was too much part of her simply to no longer be. She could no more lose its active presence than she could stop loving me and Chris. It trumped everything, swallowing the sadness of Em's absence. A love like that only stops if you let it.

★   ★   ★

Mum had outdone herself this year. Every item of clothing I had ever coveted, she had bought for me. She'd come up with books I hadn't even mentioned to her, and a DVD of every film Amber and I had ever watched together.

On the table stood a jug of Buck's Fizz that she and Chris polished off in pretty much one gulp.

'Pace yourself, big lad. It's going to be a long day,' Mum said as he downed his third glass just as I unwrapped the biggest present — a record player — and a stack of my favourite albums on vinyl.

'My turn!' Chris said when I was finished. He had fewer boxes than I did. But they were all bigger.

He opened the first one and there was nothing inside.

'Um, Mum . . . ' he said.

'Oops!' she said, swallowing a mince pie whole without chewing.

Chris opened the second and the third box and each held just more and more wrapping.

'Julie, Christmas is no time for jokes. Look at the poor lad's face!' Grandma said. Mum just laughed gleefully at his mounting frustration, like the villainous matriarch in a Roald Dahl story. I suspect a TV guide would describe her idea of comedy as 'dark', or, at very best, 'alternative'.

'You've missed one, by the way,' she said, pointing to the edge of another parcel poking out from beneath a cushion.

'If this is a lump of coal, I'm emigrating . . . just saying,' said Chris, teasing open the wrapping.

The box inside dropped on to the sofa. It was long and velvety, the sort of thing that usually has a diamond necklace inside. Chris popped the lid and then stood up even faster than when he had been electrocuted.

'OH, YOU HAVEN'T?' he said, launching himself at Mum who was practically in hysterics.

'Look at your little face . . . ' she said, squeezing his cheeks before he dashed out and threw open the front door.

'Come on, handsome,' Mum said, helping me to my feet and leading me after him. 'Your time will come.'

'What is it?' Grandma yelled as she hobbled after us all.

Instead of Mum's car being in the garage, a

new car for Chris stood in its place. She'd managed to put a ribbon around it and had tied a huge gift tag to the wing mirror.

'*Oh, you're good!*' Chris said, rushing over to look at the car, then rushing back to hug Mum.

'Merry Christmas, my love,' she said, giving him a kiss on the cheek. 'I don't know what I'd do without you.'

'Have a disposable income, probably,' he said, and Mum laughed as he opened the doors in turn and threw himself into the driver's seat, pulling down visors and checking the glove box.

'By the way, you're picking up Colette at half-ten, so have a coffee and put something in your stomach before you go,' Mum yelled, but Chris just cranked up the radio as we made our way back inside and left him alone with his favourite new toy.

'You've gone soft,' Grandma said to Mum as we sat back down with bacon sandwiches while they both opened their presents.

'It's a passing phase,' Mum said.

★ ★ ★

While Chris went to get the Spratts, Mum made me give her a hand in the kitchen.

'Put those nuts in that nice bowl I got,' she

275

said. Grandma was in the front room watching *Miracle on 34th Street*, with a bottle of Bailey's and a box of Milk Tray, and Mum was fussing about, jamming the Jurassic Turkey into the oven and fretting about cranberries and stuffing.

'You should relax,' I told her.

'I will,' she said, sitting down next to me. 'I just want it to be perfect, you know, after . . . *everything*.'

'It is,' I said, and kissed her on the cheek. 'Thanks for Christmas.'

'You're very welcome, my love,' Mum said, mixing two Snowballs and handing one to me.

'I do need to talk to you, though, Francis. You know, about Amber being here.' I drank my cocktail in silence, terrified that Mum would try to finish the sex discussion she'd never really had with me.

'You will just go easy while they're here? I think she's only coming so you're not disappointed.'

'And because we're in love,' I reminded her.

'And that. But you know what I mean, Francis. She's really not doing too great at the moment, so let's just take today as it comes, yeah?'

I was going to answer but at that moment

the door flew open and we were greeted by Colette's rendition of 'Good King Wenceslas'.

In the front room Grandma turned up the volume of the TV. Mum shut the kitchen door.

'Season's greetings!' Colette called, hugging each of us in turn. Even Mum didn't try to stop her, which was testament either to Christmas spirit or else wine for breakfast. 'I expect you're exhausted, what with all the chopping and peeling?'

It was Amber who looked exhausted, I thought, like a cheap photocopy of herself, but she gave me a wink and even a quick kiss on the cheek when she thought no one was looking.

'Oh, I don't do chopping,' Mum said, preparing a tray of drinks to take into the living room.

'Is that the boys' job?'

'Marks and Spencer's,' Mum said, leading everyone into the front room.

★   ★   ★

Colette had made presents for everybody, including Grandma.

'From the heart,' she said as she doled out the gifts.

'Isn't that champion?' Grandma said

277

unconvincingly as she dropped her handmade candle into one of her gift bags. Mum was given a bottle of elderflower wine, Chris a woodwork CD rack that was actually quite decent.

'You're a dark horse, you, Colette,' Mum said, eyeing up Chris's gift. 'You know, if you ever wanted to start selling these, I could have you a website up in no time.'

'Oh, no, it's all for love, and of course fun. We had quite a time with the glue gun and paints!'

'It was literally non-stop,' Amber said, and Mum gave her a sly smile.

Mum had bought a dozen books and an art set the size of a snooker table for Olivia. For Amber she'd pulled some strings and got a year's free pass to a cinema in town that showed mostly black-and-white or foreign films. Chris had made her a CD of alternative Christmas songs and even designed a label for it in her own special font. On it he'd written 'Have Yourself A NMErry Little Christmas'.

'That's some priceless punning,' she said, handing him the homemade biscuits that constituted the second half of his present.

'*And what did you two get each other?*' he asked with a meaningful glance at us both.

'Leave them alone,' Mum said, filling up

everybody's glasses. 'They can do theirs later if they like.'

The room filled with noise again. Even though there were only seven of us there seemed to be a thousand different conversations happening at once. Through the background sound, as Mum went over to fill up Amber's glass they had a secret chat. Amber nodded, and Mum gave her a stealth hug before dashing off to check on the parsnips.

Downstairs she and Colette wailed along to Christmas carols as they put the final touches to the meal. Chris said his main present to me would be a free half-hour, so he cracked open the box of parlour games for Olivia and Grandma while Amber and I snuck off to my room.

'Merry Christmas,' she said, giving me a proper kiss once I'd helped her up the stairs.

'Are you enjoying yourself? Did you like the tree? It's as good as the one on the box. I made Chris do it three different times before it was right.' Amber nodded and we went into my bedroom for the very first time.

I started to wonder if she felt the same way as I'd done when I first visited her house. Whether she had scanned photographs and evidence of my past to try and flesh out her picture of me. Or if I was behaving differently on my home territory. We'd hardly had a chance to speak properly, between the unwrapping of presents and the wall of sound that rose when two families collided. Also Amber seemed suddenly quieter, more delicate. Like she was no longer so sure she could take on the whole world in a fight, and win.

'Santa Baby . . . ' she said, taking the presents I'd bought for her.

The first was a book of love poems that I know she pretended to like more than she did, which did not surprise me. I was the heart and Amber was the head of our relationship, this was long established. But she loved her necklace: a pewter Magic 8 ball that she put on straight away.

'And it's only got one response written on the bottom — Yes — so it always gives a good answer,' I said happily.

'What if you ask it a bad question, though?'

'I didn't think that bit through. But it would be a big help if you didn't, if that's OK?'

'I promise to treat it with the respect and optimism it deserves,' Amber said, leaning forward to kiss me again.

'I feel bad now,' she said, hauling my present from her up on to the bed. It was big and rectangular and wrapped in brown paper like wartime rations. 'I didn't really spend anything,' she said, teasing her necklace between her fingers. I opened the present slowly, the huge square of starched paper coming off in one rewarding sheet.

She had given me her whole history, or just about. Every scrap of paper she'd had pinned above her bed in hospital had been glued to sheets of card, all of them stacked neatly and bound together with brown twine, and on each page she had written a paragraph, like at an art exhibition, about why every piece was special to her.

'It was either that or a laptop,' she said with an unusually nervous laugh.

'It's the nicest thing anyone's ever given me.'

'You wouldn't be saying that if you'd got a car,' Amber said. 'Here, I added a new one too,' she said, peeling back a stack of pages until she reached what she was looking for. On this piece of card was a bus ticket from her ride to the hospital, an empty Toblerone packet and a sketch of my face.

'It's from the first day we met. I stole the chocolate wrapper from your bin that day you got locked in the toilet,' she said, tarnishing the moment somewhat. 'Just so you remember.'

'I'd remember anyway. But I love it. And I love you . . . ' I said, trying not to cry. 'And I know it makes you uncomfortable to hear it, and you'll say something nasty just so you don't feel shy, but it's true and I can't not say it. So there it is. You're the only actual friend I've ever had that I'm not related to, and I know that's weird, and it's even weirder that I fancy you so much. And I know I text you all the time even when I know you should be resting, but I just get scared sometimes that you won't get better. And then I get scared that you *will* get better and realise you could have anyone else in the world that you wanted, and I hate myself for thinking that, and . . . '

Amber leaned in and kissed me to shut me up. It worked. I can't say I wasn't relieved.

'You've got nothing to worry about on that front,' she said, with such conviction that I immediately felt stupid for being so dramatic. 'And in case you haven't noticed, I've hardly been inundated with visitors. Or phone calls. Or gentlemen callers, for that matter.'

'That's because you never stop snarling.'

'I stop for you,' she said, 'sometimes.'

She teased her fingers around mine and I held hers, pulling her arm farther and farther from her body until she was forced to lean close to me, with her boobs pressing against my chest.

'Give it up, wise guy,' she said, pulling our hands back to her side of the bed. Amber had surprising upper body strength. 'You won't win this,' she warned.

We sat in silence for a while, staring up at the star mobile that had hung above my bed for as long as I could remember.

'Maybe fifteen's just not our time,' I said eventually, pulling our joined fists to my lips and kissing the knuckle of her middle finger.

'Maybe it has to be,' she said, kissing me back.

Just when things were starting to get interesting there was a knock at the door.

'There goes that moment,' she said, releasing her hand from mine. '*Entry granted*,' she yelled unenthusiastically.

Chris came into my room, making a big show of covering his eyes with one hand.

'Time's up, I'm afraid. I've done Charades, the Minister's Cat, and we nearly cremated Grandma when Olivia spilled the Snap Dragon bowl. I've done my brotherly duty, guys, time to face the music again.'

'You've done a fine job, young Wootton. You'll get your reward in heaven,' said Amber, pulling me up from the bed.

★ ★ ★

Lunch was a triumph. Nobody commented that the turkey was a bit dry and the vegetables a bit watery. At Christmas you don't notice the finer details, like how the house is a bit hot and the hats tickle your head. You get swept up in the big picture. And besides, what we lacked in quality we made up for in quantity. We all wore hats and made jokes, and the pudding was so big that when we set it on fire everyone pushed their seats back for fear of being incinerated.

'Of course . . . ' Colette was saying — she'd already had three glasses of Mum's special mulled wine, which is a bit like normal mulled wine but with brandy in it, and had moved on to champagne — ' . . . Amber wouldn't sleep at all throughout the night. She'd wail and yell and I'd be at my wits' end. I exhausted myself trying to lull her. Then her dad would come home from night shift, lift her to his chest, and . . . ' Colette's voice rose an octave and she held her hand to her mouth. Everyone went quiet.

'Don't, Mum,' Amber said, abandoning her uneaten pudding. 'Not today.'

'Come on,' Mum said, uncorking the bottle of homemade elderflower wine and topping up her glass. 'Any port in a storm, eh? Port . . . *port*? Oh, I should have been on the stage,' she said, taking a sniff of the wine and shrugging as she slugged it back.

Colette smiled and took a sip of her own drink, wiping her eyes with her napkin.

'Ask Mum about Christian,' Amber said with a secret sort of smile.

'No, you'll make me blush!' Colette cried.

'The hippy with the goatee?' Mum asked. At one point on the unit Christian had attempted to do a family therapy session, only Mum and Chris started rowing. Christian had to leave the room and when he came back I could tell he'd been crying. He didn't try again after that.

'Oh, he has been a help. He's got a good soul, that man,' Colette said.

'I reckon he'd be a bit of all right if you gave him a good wash and a shave,' Mum said. 'Bit scrawny, but I'm sure you could toughen him up.'

'Well, I quite like the gentle type . . . ' Colette giggled.

'You are a dark horse all right. Let's us girls have a chat after dinner. I reckon I could match you tit for tat,' Mum said, making Colette go all coy.

When Grandma asked if this meant Mum was courting again, she just shrugged and tapped the side of her nose.

★   ★   ★

After dinner Mum and Colette sat in the kitchen talking about menfolk while Chris, Olivia and

Grandma passed out on the sofa in front of *The Snowman*. Amber and I lay on the couch in the conservatory, curled around one another under two blankets while we listened to the crackling sound of the snow melting on the glass. She had turned the TV on but I'd turned it back off. I could feel Christmas passing too fast and wanted to concentrate hard, like I did on the last morsel of pudding dissolving in my mouth. The worst part of Christmas is that it ends. That practically the day after, everyone carries on as if nothing else ever happens. You're expected to go back to your normal life, eat normal food, not receive presents or celebrate or be jolly and wear stupid clothing, just because the moment's passed.

Not this year, though. This year I intended to stretch out Christmas for ever. With the TV on we could have lost a whole hour to *Morecambe and Wise* repeats without even realising it.

Amber kept nodding off against my chest and waking herself up. For once I was happy not to speak to her, just lie there and hold her instead.

'I'm going back into hospital after Christmas,' she said, sleepily, without looking up at me.

'Why?' I asked.

Amber didn't say anything at first. I could

feel my heartbeat getting quicker and more intense, like it was trying to thrash its way out of my chest. With Amber I sometimes felt the way I did after I'd missed a day or two of school, and on my return it seemed as though everybody had skipped an entire academic year, knowing the answers to questions I didn't even understand. Amber was in control in a way I never would be. She took everything in her stride. She always knew what to say to people; always knew exactly how much to care, and how much to show. Compared to her I felt like I'd been given an instruction manual with half the pages missing. To Amber life made sense; everything had context, relevance. To me most things seemed to forecast the impending apocalypse. You'd think her influence would have had a stabilising effect on my sensibilities. In reality it just meant I had to worry for us both.

'I'm letting you know,' she said eventually, 'so you don't wonder why I'm not about.'

I told her I'd visit her, but Amber said no.

'I need to go in on my own this time, Francis. I need you to understand that.'

Had she not been so drowsy and vulnerable this news would most certainly have led to our second real row. I was a man destroyed.

'But I don't! We're a team.'

'I know. And we are. But this is something I need you to do for me. I need you not to text me, and I need you not to visit. And I need you to let me be. It doesn't change anything between us.'

'Well, I'm coming anyway,' I said.

'Then I'll never forgive you.'

I suddenly felt like I was having a Soap Opera Christmas, where everyone is miserable and everything always explodes and people cry next to broken trees while the radio plays a tinny version of 'Stay Another Day'.

'Have I done something wrong?' I asked.

Amber laughed slightly and rubbed my chest.

'No,' she said, 'you did everything right. Just . . . do this, for me. Everything's still the same between us. But I have to do this bit on my own. OK?'

It certainly was not.

'My dad came back, you know?' I said. Partly because I hadn't told Amber yet, and we told each other everything. And partly to try to make her feel sorry for me, and let me visit her.

'Hmmm. How awful,' she said, although I could tell she was falling asleep again. 'Did he upset you?'

I said no.

'Hmmmm. Is he coming back?'

I said no.

'Hmmmmmm. Do you hate him?'

I said no.

'Hmmmmm,' she said, her head dipping into the crease of my shoulder. 'Good,' she said, almost in a whisper. 'Life's too short.'

15

The snow was practically gone by Boxing Day. It was as though it had arranged a suicide pact with Christmas itself. Patches of street began to poke through the white, like mould on bread. By the first week of the New Year everything looked like it had always done, only wetter and sadder, like yesterday's packed lunch.

Even the tree in the front room started to seem slightly desperate once Mum had relieved it of most of the cards and all of the presents. During my first year in Seniors I had turned up to our end-of-term disco in a dinner jacket and black tie, so I knew how it felt. It didn't help that Chris had eaten every last one of the edible decorations and, after coming home on New Year's Day still steaming drunk, half a plastic one too.

'It's bad luck after the fifth,' Grandma would warn Mum every time she came round, pointing at the limp tree.

'I'm working on the hunch I'll come back one day and the lads will have taken it down as a thank you for Christmas,' Mum told her.

Grandma made her Good Luck With That One face and carried on knitting.

Amber stuck to her word even if I hadn't stuck to mine. I would text her every day, to no response. Her phone was almost permanently switched off. Even when I tried ringing Colette she was never at the house. I began to carry my mobile everywhere with me, like it was a new baby that needed constant attention. I'd even wrap it in a sandwich bag and rest it on the toilet when I had a bath, lest it spring to life while I wasn't looking and Amber would be left thinking I didn't care.

'Give her time,' Mum would say, before skipping on to a different subject.

'I don't think the pain of a broken heart is one I will survive,' I said, lying across the upstairs landing so that everybody would notice my plight.

Grandma stepped over me on the way to the bathroom and muttered something about Alka-Seltzer. Mum would give me a sly kick every time she hopped over my soon-to-be corpse and tell me to stop being so melodramatic.

Worse still was that as well as an AWOL lover I was also being faced with the threat of an imminent return to school.

'Half-days at first. Maybe every other day,' Mum said as she ironed my underwear in the kitchen. She'd even ironed my school uniform and hung it on the door of my wardrobe, like a skull's head on a writer's desk; a constant reminder of exactly where I was heading.

'But what if Amber gets better?' I said. 'Or worse?' Mum didn't reply. 'The school will have to know about the circumstances in case I need to leave halfway through a lesson.'

'What time's Chris coming?' Mum asked, checking her watch. Mum is not an accomplished listener, like I am. She can be quite emotionally distant. I suspect Dad has something to do with this, as well as the fact that she grew up on a street where lots of people now take drugs and go to the shops in their slippers and dressing gowns. Hers was not a 'talking' environment.

The truth was that I knew something bad was happening. Chris was being overly sympathetic: letting me choose what music to listen to or what films to watch, instead of playing couch commando like he usually did. Even Mum kept giving me secret glances, like she had done before — when she knew I wasn't well and suspected what was coming, but hadn't yet been given the diagnosis. It was the look she had given me when she'd wanted everything to be different. When she didn't want to admit what was probably true.

I was getting better but Amber didn't seem to be. The truth was she was getting worse.

The truth was that I think she knew it. Worst of all the truth was that at first, as upsetting as the thought of her being ill was for me, all I could really think about was where this would leave us vis-à-vis being in love.

The superstitions I had affected soon became rituals that I would perform in an attempt at some cosmic cure. Every morning I would open Amber's Christmas present to me and display the laminated cards on the floor, in chronological order, for the whole day. Then each evening I would pack them away, still in order, and return them to my bedside table before kissing the windowpane goodnight.

I would listen only to songs we had listened to together. I would listen to each song until the end. Even if I needed the toilet or to throw up, I would simply gird the threatening orifice until the final bar had faded. And I would leave the room only in the silent moments between songs, lest one start and have to be cut short at its peak.

For a while I almost stopped speaking to Mum. I was scared she might lie to me. Or, worse, that she might tell me the truth and I might not like it. She'd been busy since Christmas anyway; out of the house more, leaving Chris and Grandma to hold the fort while she gallivanted elsewhere in my time of need.

She had arranged for Chris to take me to the January sales in his new car even though it would have been quicker getting the bus.

We spent forty-five minutes looking for a parking spot, then at least half an hour at each till. Chris nearly got into a fight with two bigger lads over a pair of jeans he'd had his eye on. Nothing I had earmarked was in my size, but I didn't let that stop me. All that mattered was that it was cheap and I had money. I got a pair of trainers two sizes too big, jeans that ended an inch above my ankles, and a T-shirt I hated but which came from a shop I liked and was seventy-five percent off, so it seemed a false economy not to buy it.

'You look like you're on day release,' Chris said as we made our way back to the car. I could barely hear him. Every ounce of my concentration was going into not tripping over in my stupid clown feet. I had made the unwise decision to have my old clothes bagged and wear my fancy new finds home, so that I could debut my new look to the world at large. The reaction had been mixed at best, but often Tyne and Wear was unable to keep up with my style savvy so I didn't let it dishearten me.

Fiona had texted telling Chris that if he didn't turn up with food within fifteen minutes she would change the locks, so he dropped me off outside the house.

'You know,' he said, as I was getting out of the car without bending my legs (the jeans were somewhat inhibiting), 'if you ever need to talk or anything, Frankie, I'm always here.'

★ ★ ★

When I got inside the house I could hear music playing from the front room. I shouted for Mum to come and look at my edgy new attire.

'You won't believe it was all at least half-price!' I yelled to no response, clomping through the hall in trainers that kept trying to fly from my feet.

I heard the music dip to its lowest setting, which meant that Mum was preparing herself for my grand entrance. I walked proudly into the living room, feeling sprightly at having achieved an iconic look on such a measly budget, only to be deflated by a sight so terrifying I could literally feel the colour drain from my face.

'Hello there, young man,' said DS Bradshaw from the couch. Only he wasn't dressed as a policeman today, he was in jeans and a smart/casual shirt that made him look oddly vulnerable. I could probably beat him in a fight if it came to it, I thought.

And it probably would come to a fight.

'Oh, Francis, I didn't hear you come in,' Mum said, as close to blushing as she ever got. She had on her black dress. Not her going out one. The one she wore for things like parents' evening when she wanted people to know she'd done all right for herself but didn't like to brag.

I did not say a word.

'Hope you've been keeping your nose clean,' DS Bradshaw said, trying to be jovial as he sipped a bottle of beer. I wondered what the police force would make of the fact that he was drinking alcohol at barely half-past three in the afternoon. I would inform them at the first given opportunity, and also of his professional misconduct re Mum.

'Come on, let's get you sorted out,' she said, hurrying me out of the front room and into the kitchen.

'Mum . . . ' I hissed, turning on the radio so that our conversation could not be overheard ' . . . *not cool.*'

'Oh, grow up, Frankie,' she said, buttering two pieces of bread without any of the care or love she usually demonstrated while performing such tasks. This was obviously the effect another man had on our family unit. It must be stopped. 'You overreact to everything. Dennis is just an old friend.'

'An *old sex friend*,' I said, and Mum gave a threatening raise of her eyebrows. 'Anyway it's not *Dennis*. It's *DS BRADSHAW* . . . The man who incarcerated me for drugs and almost ruined my life!'

'For God's sake,' she said, slapping a wet sliver of ham on to my sandwich and practically slamming it down on the plate, 'it's just a drink with a friend, which is something I'm pretty short on these days.'

'You've got the girls.'

'That's different.'

'And what about Dad?'

'He made his bed, Francis, I should be able to do whatever the hell I like in mine.'

More than losing my virginity, more than cancer, more even than the time I saw a lady fall over in the street and didn't laugh, this was the exact moment I felt the last shred of my childhood disintegrate. With that comment from my mother I became a man, and the cruelty of the adult world hit me full force.

I looked down at the guilt sandwich Mum had made me and suddenly felt very old.

'I thought you said you were just friends? And you and Dad aren't even properly divorced. It's bigamy. You could go to jail, and so could he . . . '

'I don't know where you get this stuff from Francis . . . '

297

' . . . plus I know what they do to coppers when they get sent down. I saw it on *Bad Girls*.'

'*Oh, God, where are we now in the world?*' Mum asked, pouring me a glass of water and handing me my tablets. 'Like it or lump it, Frankie, it is what it is. Now, you can either shut up, buck up, and get on with it. Or you can sit and sulk. We can talk about it later. Or we can act like it never happened. But either way, for me, for everything I've ever done for you, just give it a rest and let us finish our drink, eh?'

I shrugged. Meaning I had not yet made up my mind about Mum's illicit affair. She gave my head a paltry stroke and made her way back into the front room. I was left alone to my loveless ham sandwich, which caught on the back of my throat like a lie.

Chris arrived within fifteen minutes of me texting him for emergency backup. I snuck him in through the kitchen door so that Mum wouldn't hear him come in.

'This is priceless,' he whispered as he made his way into the front room.

I sat and listened from the kitchen, waiting for the inevitable fireworks. I heard him say hi, in an overly enthusiastic way, and Mum groan.

'Did *he* put you up to this?' she said in her

fed-up tone of voice.

It went quiet for a while. For nearly ten minutes I sat and tried in vain to listen to the conversation. Chris would no doubt be berating them both for being so inconsiderate in the face of my heartache. He was probably insisting that DS Bradshaw vacate the premises immediately, and brandishing a poker or similar blunt instrument.

Eventually the voices grew louder. Then out of nowhere came laughter.

I moved closer to the kitchen door, but still couldn't hear properly. So I made my way across the hallway, crawling on my hands and knees so that my footsteps would not give my presence away.

I crouched on all fours outside the front-room door. Chris was telling a story. Mum was laughing. DS Bradshaw was silent. I had my ear pressed against the lowest panel when the door flew open and I found myself eyeing Mum's knees.

'What the hell are you doing there, Francis?' she asked.

'Looking for a contact lens.'

'You don't wear contacts. Get up.'

'Not one of mine,' I said as Mum hauled me to my feet, 'Amber's.'

'She doesn't wear contacts either.'

'Not since she lost it,' I said, without even

299

having to pause for thought. I am quite adept at thinking on my feet.

'Dennis was just leaving,' Mum said as DS Bradshaw put on his coat. I shrugged and went to sit down next to Chris, who shook his head.

'Nice to meet you, Christopher,' the visitor said, shaking his hand. Chris even stood up to do it. He was obviously more fearful of authority than I was. I refused to let myself be intimidated by The Man.

'And, Frankie, glad to see you on the mend. You keep yourself out of bother, for your mam's sake,' he said.

Mum saw him to the front door and stood there for upwards of three minutes. There was whispering and laughter — no doubt about me — and all the while an icy blast blew through the front passage and into the living room, threatening us all with pneumonia or worse.

'What is your problem?' Chris asked me. 'She's happy, can't you see that?'

'He's probably trying to trick her. He can't be trusted,' I said, confident in my diagnosis of the situation.

'Just lay off.'

Chris didn't side with Mum. He never sided with Mum. The car had obviously been her attempt to bribe him over to her side from mine. I hated that car.

'We'll see.'

'Be cool, Francis, this is a big deal for her.'

'Fine,' I said, as Mum came back into the front room. 'But I'm not happy.'

'*Not a word*,' she said, clearing away.

'I like him,' Chris said as Mum picked up the bowl of crisps and the two empty beer bottles that Dennis had been drinking from. While she was tidying she had a stupid sort of smile on her face. The type you get at school when someone hands you a note but you can't laugh out loud.

'Well, thank you,' she said, tipping the rest of the wine into a small glass.

'He's all right,' I said, eventually. 'I suppose.'

Mum put all the things on to a tray and hoisted it off the coffee table.

'You'll always be my guy, Francis. Just you remember that,' she said, kissing me on the head before making her way to the kitchen.

★   ★   ★

In the weeks after DS Bradshaw came into our home Mum started behaving suspiciously. She would take phone calls while locked in the bathroom, with the taps running, sometimes for up to an hour. I'd time her with the stopwatch on my phone.

More than once she left the house, too, in the middle of the night, then denied all knowledge of her nocturnal activities the following morning.

'I watched you leave,' I told her while I was making my way through my Ready Brek, having jotted down a brief timescale on the notepad I'd bought to take on to the unit.

'It must have been a dream,' she said, and seemed unwilling to consider the concrete evidence in the form of my Diary of Observations.

Even Chris became distant with me. When I told him about Mum's activities he would simply shrug off my concerns and try to change the subject.

'I think she might be running drugs,' I said eventually, feeling lighter for having voiced my deepest fear.

'Well, if she was only gone an hour and twenty-two minutes then I very much doubt she could have made it to Colombia and back,' Fiona said, when I tried to make an ally of her too.

That night, in the bath, I lay back and dragged my hands through the proud stubs of hair that had begun to sprout from my head. I poured a glob of shampoo into my palm, the size of a fifty-pence piece, as the bottle recommended, and lathered my soon-to-be mane.

Just as I was about to rinse and repeat my phone buzzed and began to jerk wildly on the toilet lid.

I grabbed the sandwich bag and felt the zip-lock slip between my soapy fingers twice as I furiously tried to yank it aside.

I managed to unfurl my phone from its wetsuit and felt a shiver as I saw the two words I'd been dreaming of for weeks:

Message Received

Then, in bleak slow motion, the phone slipped from my lubed hand and sank straight to the bottom of the bathtub. The 'crack' it made against the porcelain seemed to vibrate through my whole body.

I retrieved it from its watery grave and dirty water trickled from the battery slot. The screen was blank, each button unresponsive.

I yelled for Mum, pulling on my clothes without drying myself. She didn't answer. Her bathroom door was locked, but I could hear that she was on the phone.

'Mum, there's been an emergency!'

'*Hold on one second . . .* ' I heard her say down the line. 'Are you OK?' she called to me.

'My phone dropped in the bath and Amber texted me and I need it sorted *now*.'

303

There was a long pause. Mum said something else down the phone and then shouted through the door again.

'Chris is downstairs. He'll sort it for you.'

'But I need it now,' I called. 'It's an emergency.'

'Francis,' Mum said, 'I'm warning you. *Not now*.'

Even if the phone was a lost cause, one thing I knew for certain was that Mum's campaign of deceit was coming to an end. She was no match for me when it came to cunning and innovation.

All the laptops in our house had wireless internet. Only the battered old PC in the spare bedroom was dial-up. If you tried to connect it to the internet when someone was on the phone their conversation would play out through the furry speakers that slotted into the monitor.

Mum would rue the day she'd tried to get one over on me, I thought as I turned on the machine. It coughed and spluttered and then gave the old-fashioned six-bar refrain that meant Microsoft was welcoming you to its world. Three different virus warnings sprang on to the screen but I ignored them, like an action hero wading through heavy fire to defeat the enemy.

I clicked on to the internet and pressed

connect, turning the speakers to their lowest volume.

'*I know . . .*' I heard Mum say through the speakers. Someone was crying down the line, a woman, but I couldn't hear who ' *. . . and I'll have my mobile on. It's only down the road, so if you need anything, anything at all, you just get in touch.*'

There was a long silence before a woman's familiar voice answered her.

'*Thank you, Julie.*'

It was Colette.

The line went dead.

★ ★ ★

'What's going on?' I asked Chris. He was sitting at the kitchen table and looked the way he did when he had a hangover, all red-eyed and distant.

'What?' he said, glancing up at me. 'Frankie, you're soaking wet, you'll catch your death . . . '

I told him about the text, about the phone/bath disaster, and about Mum's secret conversations with Colette, but Mum interrupted us before he'd had a chance to reply.

'Right, lads, change of plan.' Mum said that she had rung school and postponed my return. Instead she had arranged a trip to see

Aunty Carol in York.

Aunty Carol is not my real aunty, I just call her that because she has known me since I was a baby and Mum says it makes her feel special. She used to live across the road from us, and had four cats and no husband but two children who moved down south and didn't visit very often. Mum used to take her shopping once a week. Aunty Carol met a man on the Internet and moved to Yorkshire to live with him and help him make pottery bowls that they sell at markets. We have visited her just three times. Once when Emma died. Once when Dad left. And once when the doctors said Granddad wasn't going to get better.

'No,' I said. 'Amber texted me. She's better.'

'The text wasn't from Amber,' Mum said.

'Nobody else texts me.'

'He knows you were on the phone to Colette,' Chris said, rubbing his hand across his mouth.

'I demand answers!' I said, holding up my sodden mobile for dramatic effect.

'Give us a minute, love,' Mum said to Chris.

★ ★ ★

'I'm so proud of you,' she said to me once my brother had shut himself in the conservatory. She'd sat down next to me and was forcing a smile. 'My brave lad.'

I shrugged.

'You're coming on in leaps and bounds, you know. You're looking better. Getting better. That's really all we need to be thinking about at the moment.'

'I thought that was all we *were* thinking about?'

Mum nodded then let out a long, single sigh of exhaustion, like a bouncy castle being burst. Looking down at the table, she began to explain.

'Francis, do you know what 'palliative' means?'

I said I did, because I hated it when she knew what words meant and I didn't. Mum only got three O-levels. With over nine mock GCSEs at grades A-C I was already her intellectual superior and didn't want her getting ideas above her station.

'What exactly do you think it means?' she asked me.

I guessed at something to do with colour.

Mum shook her head.

'Palliative means they make you comfortable when you're unwell.'

'Like when I was on the unit?'

'No, love,' she said, shaking her head. 'It means they make you comfortable because that's all they can do. Because there's nothing else to try. They make you comfortable because they can't make you better.'

'What's that got to do with anything?'

'Oh, sweetheart,' Mum said, still not answering my question. The question I hadn't really needed to ask in the first place. When Granddad was ill one last time they took the tubes out of his nose and left him in his hospital bed until he was quiet and still. Until he just stopped. 'Comfortable' was the word everybody kept using then. I never understood why nobody thought to question this. How could they know that? What if he was actually in pain? What if he was fighting it, desperately trying to find the energy to ask us to plug him back into the machines and the drips and the medicine that they'd fed straight into his veins?

'Do you mean Amber?' I said. Mum nodded. 'But she's getting better. She texted me.'

'No, sweetheart,' Mum said in a whisper.

'I love her,' I said.

'Francis, you're only fifteen . . . '

I think there was probably an end to the sentence but I didn't give her the chance.

'What do you know about anything

308

anyway? You haven't even got A-levels. And I *do* love Amber and I know I mean it. You wouldn't even understand because if you'd loved Dad more he probably wouldn't have left you in the first place . . . ' I said through tears.

I went on and on like this for minutes, until I had spoken so much I had to inhale two desperate lungfuls of air that made me feel faint. I wanted to hurt Mum. I wanted everything I said to stab straight through her, so she'd double over in agony and feel as ruined as I did. But she didn't. She didn't even react. Everything I said seemed to bounce off her like chucked balls of newspaper.

'Come here,' she said, trying to hug me.

'No.'

I could hardly see through the tears. The chair fell over as I stood up and made a sound like lightning striking the kitchen floor.

'Francis . . . ' Mum said as I left. 'Francis, where are you going? Francis . . . come back!' she yelled.

I could hear Chris calling my name from the conservatory, but ran to my room and barricaded the door shut.

I dried myself, and changed, and filled my pockets with the essentials I needed. Then I listened carefully until I heard the conservatory door open and shut. This was my moment.

The taxi dropped me off outside the hospital and I made my way to the unit where Jackie was at the nurses' station.

I told her I was there to see Amber, trying to crane my neck to see if she was inside.

Jackie nodded and gave me a hug, and I took the opportunity to peek over her shoulder to see if I could spot Amber. Her bed was empty. Kelly was asleep and a stranger was in the bed that had once been mine.

'She's not on the unit any more,' Jackie said. 'Does your mam know you're here?'

'Yes,' I said. 'She dropped me off.'

'All right then,' Jackie said, 'follow me.'

Amber's room was square and empty. The walls were white, and chipped towards the ceiling. There were no posters or photographs, no keepsakes or mementos. There wasn't even a bedside table, just one machine that beeped and hissed, attached to her thin arm by a tube.

Colette didn't say anything when I walked in. I think she knew I was coming. She took Olivia by the hand, kissed Amber on the forehead, and walked slowly past me into the corridor.

'There's a button by the bed, if you need anything,' Jackie said, closing the door behind her.

Amber's skin hung from her like a sheet thrown over a coat rack, and her chest heaved up and down with each tiny breath she took.

'Where's my dad?' she asked weakly as I sat down beside the bed, terrified to touch her.

I said I didn't know, because that was the truth. Amber seemed to recognise my voice. She rolled her head and looked straight into my eyes, before turning her gaze back towards the ceiling and scrunching up her face tightly as she drew in one long, high-pitched breath.

I said her name out loud, and her face relaxed a little. I said it again.

'Amber, I need you to get up,' I said, stretching my hand towards her arm. I stroked my fingers across her cool skin, trying to warm her up without pressing too hard, like an apple straight from the fridge. I ran my fingers up her arms and down towards her hand that was so pale it was virtually camouflaged against the bedspread.

'Amber, I know you're tired,' I whispered, 'and that you're unwell. But if you could just get up, just for a bit, I think you'd see things differently.'

She turned to look at me and tears began to form in the corners of her eyes.

'I want my hair back,' she said, with utter conviction. 'I don't want to go anywhere without my hair.'

'It grows back when you're better. Look,' I said, bending down and passing her hand across the crown of my head, letting her limp palm rest against my proud new patch of hair.

I sat up again and Amber turned her face back towards the ceiling, tears cutting down the sides of her face like condensation on a bus window.

I took a tissue from my back pocket and wiped away each one.

'The thing is, Amber, I need you to get better because I'm getting better, and the problem is I can't really remember what I ever did before I knew you. Before we were us. I know you must feel scared about being ill, but I'm starting to feel scared about getting better . . . about having to do anything without you.'

Amber closed her eyes gently and breathed in deeply while I spoke.

'And even if you don't always love me, even if we don't always know each other, I think the world will always be a more interesting place with you in it . . . so with that in mind I think what you're doing is really irresponsible,' I said, trying to claw back my breath as Amber's image became blurred by my own tears, like a firework squinted at through watering eyes.

'Please, Amber,' I whispered in her ear,

'please just get up. Prove everyone wrong one more time.'

I felt her breath on my neck, soft and uncertain like a baby's.

Amber's chest began to move in steadier, shorter bursts, like rippling tide.

Amber was designed for life. She was designed for colour and movement. She was not a girl born for the click of the camera's lens. No device could capture her, the way she was, the way she was meant to be. She was not born to be still or stationary. Without her colour she was broken; a faulty image that could never be fixed. Without her voice she was nothing. Amber was gone. At that moment it was all clear to me. Everything to come was just a formality.

When I realised there would be no answer from her, I stood up and kissed her gently on the forehead.

I whispered something in her ear and, from my back pocket, took out the lock of her hair, and slid it beneath the palm of her right hand.

★ ★ ★

Mum found me in the entrance hall on the way out of the hospital. I was half-blinded by tears and light-headed from sobbing so hard.

313

I saw her coming towards me down the corridor and tried to avoid her. I speeded up, edging my way towards the farthest wall as best I could, and nearly made it.

'Francis sweetheart,' she said, taking hold of my arm.

'Don't,' I said, pulling away, but she held on tight and dragged me towards her. I felt her wrap her arms around me, tightly, like a safety belt.

'I know . . . ' she said as both of us felt our knees give way beneath us until we were sitting on the floor ' . . . I know.'

We ended up huddled together in the hospital corridor, where we sat until I couldn't cry any more.

★ ★ ★

When we did get home Mum followed me upstairs and sat with me in silence on my bed.

'I have something to give you, Francis,' she said eventually, 'but if you think it'll upset you too much I can keep it for as long as you need me to, OK?' I nodded. 'It's from Colette,' she said, taking a thin white envelope from her handbag. 'Amber asked her to give you it. I'll leave it on your bed. But if you don't want to open it, you just remember what I said.'

Once she had gone I stood up and opened the letter. I picked along the seal with the sharpest edge of my nail scissors, so that none of the paper ripped, and carefully removed the folded white sheet from inside.

When I opened the letter hundreds of gold stars, tiny like glitter, tumbled down from the folded page on to my lap.

The handwriting was Amber's, each letter pressed hard into the page like she was shouting.

Dear Francis,
. . . Shut up and deal.
Always,
Amber

That night I slept in Mum's bed. I didn't ask. I just crawled in sometime after nine and let her wrap her arms around me from behind, drawing me towards her until our breathing became synchronised and I fell asleep, slowly but steadily, like a film fading to black.

At thirteen minutes past one in the morning our phone rang. Mum picked up, even though she didn't have to.

When someone phones that late it can only mean bad things.

And it did.

After

It's six years later and we are traipsing towards a wedding.

Can you guess whose?

I'll give you a clue. It's not actually a wedding; it's an interfaith blessing of a lifetime's commitment. The priest is actually a member of a folk band, and two of the bridesmaids (the ones who aren't Mum) are wearing tie-dyed kaftans.

Also, it's not in a church. The whole ceremony is being held in a forest.

It seems Christian wasn't as soppy as Amber always said he was, because after it happened he and Colette became acquainted in all sorts of ways that wouldn't have been legal were he any sort of doctor. They were an item by the following Christmas, and got engaged during my gap year.

Mum's voice went shrill when she found out.

Much to her pleasure, she was made responsible for the hen night. After nixing a night on the town Colette had agreed to a civilised meal at our house with some of her closest friends.

When Colette's clique arrived Mum sat them all down then locked herself in the bathroom with a bottle of rosé.

'Oh, love, it looks like a therapy group in there,' she hissed down the line at me. 'These aren't my people, Francis . . . they won't even watch *Pretty Woman* because of sexism or something.'

Things started to pick up later on and Mum must eventually have found the merits of both Colette's friends and the homemade wine they had all brought. I know this because at half-one in the morning she rang me again to sing 'Come On Eileen' with her New Best Friends For Life (her words).

On the day of the wedding Mum was going off on one before I'd even had time for breakfast. Chris and Fiona had got blind drunk the night before with Christian, and Mum couldn't get either of them out of bed.

Colette and Olivia had stayed at our house before the ceremony, at Mum's insistence. Olivia was now a year older than Amber was when I met her, a year older than Amber ever would be, and had turned into a young woman of such alarming beauty that Chris would no longer let his friends come to our house when she was there, as they spent all their time ogling her and trying to persuade her to marry them.

Fortunately she had also inherited Amber's sharpness, but in a gentler way, like a loving pastiche of the sister she sometimes worried she would one day forget.

Colette screamed blue murder when Mum tried to sneak out her make-up bag, and eventually the subject was laid to rest.

Mum got her own way about the leave-in conditioner, though, and even Colette was amazed when her hair — once wiry and unkempt, like a mop after it has been pushed under a kitchen cupboard — started to resemble something vaguely human.

DS Bradshaw, who I now call Dennis after conceding that he may not in fact be the Antichrist, had been waiting downstairs for over forty-five minutes while Mum yelled through the door of the spare room where Chris and Fiona sprawled, while she simultaneously removed the curlers from her hair.

'How's uni going?' he asked me. I had got the last train home the night before, and arrived when everyone else was in bed.

'Fine,' I said.

Only it was more than fine. It was the best time of my life. School had been a necessary evil, something to tolerate, something to survive. But everything that came after had been worth the effort, worth the misery and the panic and the Sunday Night Nausea of

Doom. Everything was how I'd always imagined it would be, but better. I spent my nights talking to interesting strangers about interesting things. I discovered friends who made me a better person. I read books that changed my life and watched films that left me so breathless that I would still be stuck to the seat long after the credits had finished rolling. I saw parts of the country, parts of the world, that at one point I couldn't even spell. I fell in and out of love on an almost daily basis, and said yes to any opportunity that came my way.

I lived.

I am now in my third year. I will graduate in the summer. I am twenty-one. It is six years since Amber.

I knocked on Mum's door as she was putting the final touches to Colette's attire. She'd made her own wedding dress out of lengths of white lace. Mum had agreed to this on the understanding that she would get to pick her own bridesmaid's outfit come the big day.

'If it's a choice between cheesecloth and death then I choose death,' she had said when Colette voiced her initial suggestion.

Mum was painting Colette's nails when she said I could come in. With a steady hand she dragged across the same shade of purple she had once given Amber, and Colette looked tearful in a happy sort of way.

'How's it going?' I asked.

Mum didn't turn around. When it came to matters of grooming she had the steely concentration of a bomb-disposal expert. Makeovers are her *Hurt Locker*.

Colette looked at me and smiled. It struck me in that moment that Amber's mouth had been just like her mother's, and suddenly I was fifteen again, and in love again, and devastated.

It took me a minute to catch my breath.

'Almost done,' Colette said.

'You look beautiful.'

'Thank you, Francis,' she said warmly.

'She's worried Christian will be too hung-over to stand up at the altar,' Mum said.

She keeps pretending it's a normal wedding, even though it isn't. There isn't an altar, for a start. The ceremony is not a religious one. It probably isn't even legal. One of Christian's friends is doing a reading, and then they are going to walk over hot coals to demonstrate their love for one another. Mum took to her bed when she first discovered it was an outdoor wedding. Grandma said she couldn't go on account of her arthritis, which was a lie, but she was going to take a taxi to the reception. In preparation for this Mum had packed three slices of ham and a Scotch egg into her bag, on the off chance Grandma made a scene when she discovered it was a vegan spread.

'Open that fizz for me, love,' Mum said, painting the last of Colette's nails.

'Only a small one for me,' Colette said with a nervy giggle.

I popped the cork and handed them both a glass.

'I've got something for you but I don't know if I should give you it now,' I said, teasing the lump through the pocket of my posh jacket.

'Oh,' Colette said, 'don't worry about me. We're tougher than we look, us Spratts. Amber didn't get it from nowhere,' she said with a laugh. Even though her nails were drying I saw Mum carefully give her hand a tight squeeze.

From my pocket I pulled out a small laminated card. On it five petals of a pansy — darkly purple, like a fresh bruise — had been pressed and roughly arranged into the shape of the flower itself.

'It was part of Amber's Christmas present to me,' I said, handing Colette the card. 'Your garden was her favourite place in the world. She told me once. I just thought it might be something nice for you to have today.'

'You're a good lad,' Mum said, giving me a hug from the footstool where she was sitting.

'Oh, Francis, what a lovely gesture!'

'I suppose it can be your something old and new, and it's near enough to blue. If you wanted to give it back it can be borrowed as well, so we're covering every base.'

'It's the perfect present,' Colette said, teasing her thumb across the fragile petals.

Mum jokingly cleared her throat and pointed to the two airline tickets on her bed. For a wedding gift she had paid for the honeymoon.

Colette laughed and so did Mum.

'I don't know what I'd have done these last few years without you. You're very dear to me, Julie Wootton.'

'Here,' Mum said, topping up her glass, 'get this down you and sort yourself out. No one wants a maudlin bride. Miss Havisham was jilted for a reason.'

I bent down and kissed Colette on the cheek.

'You do look lovely,' I said again, and left them to their drinks.

* * *

In the months after Amber's death I seemed to exist in a space there isn't yet a word for. I carried on each day, waking up, getting dressed. But I was suspended somewhere between life and death. Everything that mattered was gone, and I had been left a husk.

Colette started coming round more often. Mum would cook dinner for her and Olivia, and make sure they had plenty of food in the cupboard when she dropped them back home. Chris would sit with me for hours, sometimes talking, sometimes not.

Nothing made much difference.

Nothing made much sense.

I became half-mad.

One day in the conservatory when I was looking for a dropped fifty-pence piece I found a pair of socks that Amber had kicked off while we'd spent the evening curled on the sofa.

I carried them to my room and left them on the radiator for three months, because if I had her socks then she would have to come back and collect them, and they would be warm when she did.

I stayed up all night the next New Year's Eve. I wanted to claw at the year before, to catch it in my hands and drag myself back into it. I knew that once the New Year came Amber's death would no longer be something that was happening. It would be something that had happened. Soon she would enter the past tense, as we skipped over firsts — Christmases, birthdays, anniversaries — until eventually she was someone I had to try hard to remember, like I was looking at her through the wrong end of a telescope.

I cried as the sun rose on January the first. Amber's death felt like the last thing we could ever do together. Of course her bit of it was over. But grieving for her, loving her, missing her . . . they were all things that I still had to do. And the farther away we moved from the event, the less time I would need to devote to each one.

Life goes on.

Before long there were nights when I'd wake with a start, frantic that I had forgotten something, and eventually realise that what I hadn't done was think about Amber all day long. Days when I'd live my life without the tinnitus hum of grief acting as the screensaver to my every move.

Before long these days became weeks.

Before long these weeks became months.

Before long Amber became nothing but a memory, and a happy one at that.

*   *   *

'Oh, I am *hanging*,' Chris said, pulling at the collar of his suit, as everyone made their way downstairs.

'All right, people, we've got ten minutes before the cars get here,' Mum said, stomping down the stairs like an army corporal. 'Well, aren't you a sight?' she said to Dennis, picking a ball of fluff from the shoulder of his suit and kissing him on the cheek.

'Fiona, so help me God, if you get garlic sauce on that dress I will knock you daft,' Mum said as Fiona picked sombrely at a slice of the night before's pizza.

Everyone congregated in the front room.

'FIVE MINUTES UNTIL CARS!' Mum screamed from the top of the stairs while she hunted out her camera.

When she came down her face was clouded.

'Where in God's name is Colette?'

It appeared that in the frantic climax to the wedding preparations the whereabouts of the bride had slipped our minds completely.

'I think she went for some air,' Olivia said. 'Do you want me to go and get her?'

'No, love, your dress cost more than Chris's car. You stay put. Francis, deal with this . . . now.'

The front door had been left open. I went into the garden but couldn't see anyone there.

I walked down the street in my suit, the way I had once walked to school, and felt a phantom terror at the thought of missing the bus.

Across the road, on the benches overlooking the beach, I saw Colette sitting peacefully, alone.

'Mum says if you've done a runner she's

having your honeymoon,' I said, sitting down next to her.

'Oh,' Colette laughed. 'Just having a moment to think.'

I asked if she wanted to be left alone and she said no.

'Do you miss her all the time?' I asked.

Colette shook her head and smiled, staring out at the yawning sea that lay flat, like a sheet of gold, beneath the chilly glow of the sun.

'Every day. But I always have her here,' she said, tapping her chest. 'And here,' nodding out towards the endless stretch of ocean. 'She's for ever making herself known, that one,' Colette said with a sad laugh. 'Like always. We'll never really be rid of her, you and I.'

I put my hand in hers and she held it tightly.

'Are you happy?' I asked. She seemed to have to think for a moment, but when her answer came it was with a certainty she usually lacked.

'Oh, yes. On days like this you can't help but feel blessed,' she said as we stared out at the sea together. 'We were lucky to have had her for as long as we did. But even a day as beautiful as today must come to an end. Such a lovely day . . . Don't ever waste days like today, Francis. Don't let one second of them pass you by.'

We sat for a moment longer, hand in hand, staring out to sea, not speaking, not crying, just thinking, remembering, and smiling.

'Well, I'd imagine Julie's suitably frantic by now. What say we put her out of her misery and go and make me an honest woman?' said Colette, standing up.

I bent my elbow and let her slide her arm through mine.

'Come on,' she said, as we made our way back to the house together, 'best foot forward.'

★ ★ ★

Even Mum cried at the wedding. Chris wiped away a dignified tear when he saw me walking Colette down the aisle. I showed no such restraint. In fact, the only person who cried louder than me was Fiona, who bawled like a banshee when Colette and Christian had their first kiss as 'life partners'.

The reception lasted all night. Dennis proposed to Mum, drunkenly, and then again in the morning once they were both sober. She said no three times before eventually relenting.

'*Fine* . . . ' she said, at breakfast the next

day ' . . . but only until a better offer comes along.'

We didn't waste one second of that day. We talked about the past. We talked about the future. And we danced. And we sang. And we toasted absent friends, as the stars shone through the night sky, like Amber's last gift.

Acknowledgements

Thank you to my friends and family, particularly Dad, Nicole and Jess.

Thanks to Mandy Dobson — my first and favourite reader — for the advice, the kind words, but mostly for Sammy.

Thanks to all at Corsair and Much-in-Little.

A special thanks to Broo Doherty and Sarah Castleton.

We do hope that you have enjoyed reading this large print book.

Did you know that all of our titles are available for purchase?

We publish a wide range of high quality large print books including:
Romances, Mysteries, Classics
General Fiction
Non Fiction and Westerns

Special interest titles available in large print are:
The Little Oxford Dictionary
Music Book
Song Book
Hymn Book
Service Book

Also available from us courtesy of Oxford University Press:
Young Readers' Dictionary
(large print edition)
Young Readers' Thesaurus
(large print edition)

For further information or a free brochure, please contact us at:
Ulverscroft Large Print Books Ltd.,
The Green, Bradgate Road, Anstey,
Leicester, LE7 7FU, England.
Tel: (00 44) 0116 236 4325
Fax: (00 44) 0116 234 0205